Trisha J. Kelly

G000140901

Bromington-on-sea

A Wodehouse Mystery

Trisha J. Kelly

ISBN: **9781075382369**
ISBN-13:

Contents

Dedication

Thank you once again to my readers for supporting me and I truly appreciate your dedication. I've immensely enjoyed writing this book, the first in the Wodehouse Mysteries. I hope the characters will jump out at you too. I've come to love them all. Most of them anyway. Let's see where their journey takes them.

Bromington-on-sea

The letter arrives

Rosie was very surprised when an official letter dropped through the letterbox. Straight into the essential plastic cage on the back of the flat door. Under starters orders, Bear bounded down the laminate hallway, slipping and sliding, barking and growling at the unseen menace known as Postie.

"Too late, my precious. Mummy has it in her hands, look!" A loud bump and Bear had banged himself against the solid wooden door. The third time this week. "Silly boy! Won't you ever learn? Would you like a bone or are you..."

By the time he eventually clambered onto the battered red sofa and negotiated the arm, finally the top, the postman was several doors away. "... Happy to sit barking at the rustling wind and fresh air," Rosie finished.

"You are a daft mutt, but so cute." Bear was only a small sized pup but with the heart of a lion. He had a beige overly-round puppy head with black areas. His body was a dirty grey beige and he melted Rosie's heart. "Don't disturb Bumble, there's a good boy."

Bumble, being her grumpy ginger and black cat who took no prisoners. Although her head was buried, the banging of her bushy tail was enough to tell Rosie, Bear was treading on eggshells. Once again, the cat had claimed the fireside chair. The grubby, faded yellow cover had seen better days.

The fat letter in Rosie's hands grabbed her attention once more. It was far too official looking to be a bill, so she didn't need to add it to her growing collection. Flicking the kettle on, she discovered the tea caddy empty. All was not lost, if she banged the hard coffee long enough, she could scrape a spoonful. She checked her food situation.

Four pints of milk, half a tub of butter, ooh! six eggs, hard, but not mouldy cheese, one large tomato. Rosie found bread, soggy cornflakes and a packet of pasta. At least her pets had food for a few more days. Was it still another four days until payday? she wondered.

The calendar confirmed it. Wednesday the 24th of April. Sometimes her wages went into the bank early. Friday the 26th would be good as the 28th was a Sunday this month. Scraping the butter on her toast, she figured she can survive with what she has. Cheese omelette, pasta with melted cheese and a slurp of ketchup. Or scrambled egg, egg and soldiers, cheese on toast. Soggy cereal, the options were endless.

She plonked the letter on the worktop and browsed through Bear's options, which were considerably larger than hers. Settling for chicken, rice and peas, Rosie filled his small bowl and stirred in his favourite biscuits. With fresh water he is ready to go; as soon as his chairback mission is complete of course. Rosie leaves Bumble her favourite tuna meal, and cat milk on top of the worktop, well away from puppy interference.

She's glad she doesn't like Marmite anyway, nor jam or marmalade; well, that wasn't strictly true. Plain toast was fine. It isn't that she didn't work hard, she did. When her friend suggested tele-sales work from home it sounded great. Hours to suit in the comfort of her cosy snug. Before she sank into the doldrums her mobile phone shattered the grey thoughts racing around her mind. Bear's barking heightened above the sound of the standard ring, ring, tone.

2

"Okay Bear, I can handle it, no worries." She shut the door, drowning out his yapping and then closed the kitchen door. "Hello, Mother! How are you?" Rosie was having to shout a little. In a couple of minutes Bear would stop. "Sorry, say that again. I didn't quite catch that. A letter? Yes."

"Have you opened it, Rosie?" Her mother's sharp tone shrieked out on loudspeaker.

"No Mum, I'm just about to… wait a minute, how did you know I have a letter? Oh, you have one too. Listen, can I ring you back in a minute, when it's a little quieter. Yes… I *know* you told me not to get a dog, especially a noisy one. Yes, I *know* what else you told me. Okay, I have to go, speak in a while!"

If she didn't know better, Rosie thought Mother was actually in a good mood; first time in years. Realising little Bear was not going to shut up any time soon, she opened both doors, got back to her cold toast and stared at the letter. With a bit of luck, her cuddly friend would devour his tasty breakfast and fall asleep for a couple of hours.

Work, for Rosie, took place in the back snug. With Bear snuggled in his basket in the kitchen she could sneak away for a two-hour shift, dealing with all things concerning a certain brand of coffee- machine in her telephone voice. Mental note to herself. New pyjamas on payday. By lunch-time the world was a different place. No more work until the evening. She even had time to fit in a shower before Bear woke.

While Bear ran around with a plastic plant pot, chasing in and out of the flowers, Bumble sat on top of the fence, preening herself, washing behind her ears, majestically. Rosie cut off the mobile just as it started to ring again. Mother. Twice in one year? Oh, of course, the letter; now what's this all about? She ripped it open and sat on the kitchen stool.

Arkwright & Sullivan Solicitors? Oh dear.

Miss Rosalyn Wodehouse,

We have been instructed in the matter of the estate of the late Dorothea Wodehouse (Spinster) a paternal great aunt on your father's side of the family, recently deceased.

The reading of the will shall take place in our offices on Tuesday the 30th April at 2 p.m. As you are a beneficiary, we would be obliged of your earliest confirmation... blah, blah, blah. Rosie skipped over the rest of the details and immediately picked up her mobile phone.

"Mum? I've just opened the letter... yes I'm sorry. I had to work."

"Well, Rosalyn, I have been *trying* to tell you!" she boomed on loudspeaker.

"I know. I'm sorry. Who on earth is Dorothea Wodehouse?"

"It's a long story. Come over if you must, father will explain all. You know I'm allergic to pet fur. Have someone babysit your animals. When is good for you?"

Rosie scrabbled around in her purse. Not quite having the fare to get to her parents, she paused.

"Daddy will collect you." Two things Rosie hated, someone who could read her mind and being called Rosalyn. Three things actually, she only had one person who could help, as her mother was all too aware.

"I have a free day tomorrow. I'm sure Anna will pet-sit for me. How about eleven a.m.?"

"Sharp. Don't keep your father waiting outside. There's never anywhere to park in your small road."

Rosie closed her flat door and took the stairs two at a time. She banged on the upstairs flat. The loud music stopped.

"Rosie! I haven't seen you since yesterday! Come in, coffee?"

"Do you have tea? I can't be too long. Bear's in the garden."

"Nonsense! He can scrabble through the cat flap when he gets bored. Come and look at this, see what you think!" As usual, Anna was covered in paint, creating her latest masterpiece.

Rosie stood still and gasped. There, looking at her, were Bear and Bumble. The portrait was so lifelike, they were almost jumping out.

"Anna! It's beautiful. But… how did you keep it a secret? I'm always dropping in!"

"Ah, my friend, you look, but you don't see. Plus, I kept this one hidden in my bedroom. Now see, the final touch." She signed her name in the corner. Her famous trademark. Anna Rose.

She had a beautiful name, not like her own, Rosie thought. Well, she did have a lovely name, but it had been mis-used over the years and screeched into three syllables. Rose-ah-lyn, by a moody mother with a bad attitude. She also had a two-syllable surname, Wode-house. Anna called her friend, Rosie boo-boo, because it flowed better.

"Anna, I can't possibly afford one of your…"

"Shush, Boo-boo. Whoever mentioned anything as coarse as money. It is an early birthday present for you. I'm not giving it to you until the weekend of course! I will frame it and choose a spot for you to hang it. We don't want the sunlight fading the colours."

"It's the kindest thing anyone has ever done for me, truly. Bear and Bumble are going to love it too!"

"Hmm. It's a good job it will be behind glass by then. Your cat has very sharp claws and a wicked temper!" Anna poured tea into two china mugs. She made the best tea in the world. Leaves, not bags. Just enough milk and one posh sugar lump. She placed the tongs down and Rosie savoured the flavour. "Oh, where's my manners. Mum came yesterday, with our favourites. Here you are, Rosie, help yourself."

Small iced buns lay in two circles inside the deep Victorian tin. Yellow, pink and white. Even Bear's barking could not spoil their moment. The friends smiled and both dug hungrily into the tasty treats.

"Oh, I almost forgot, with all the excitement of the last few minutes. Would you mind very much looking after Bear for a while tomorrow? I have to go to my parents. Dad's picking me up at eleven."

"And one is allergic to fur! Of course, I can. Me and Bear have this thing. Laying all over your sofa, eating popcorn and watching chick flicks. Bumble of course, supervises our every move!"

Rose laughed at her friend who always had a twinkle in her eye. Anna was two years older and like the big sister she never had. Her friend had glorious black shiny hair, usually with a drop of paint or two, dimples, big brown eyes and an infectious personality. For the last three years they had been neighbours and they'd hit it off from day one.

Anna's flat had fascinating ornaments and furniture from around the world. She didn't flaunt them as expensive showpieces, they were handed down to her from her Nan. Rosie's flat by comparison was sparse, her choosing. She would rather struggle along than ask for anything from her parents. It came with too many conditions. Not from her dad, he was lovely, quietly spoken, too quiet. Her mother ruled the roost, the purse strings and was far too domineering. Rosie had finally saved enough for a rental deposit in a not too fussy area of town, meaning she had been allowed a kitten.

"What do you think of this? Look. It came this morning and I don't even know anything about Dorothea, it was quite a shock. Mother rang twice, they have a letter too." Rosie handed over the solicitor's letter to Anna.

"Rosie boo-boo! How very exciting. Was she a rich great aunt? Maybe you are heir to a spooky mansion or something. Don't leave me behind. What would I do without you!"

Even if Anna was pulling her leg, Rosie couldn't imagine life without her in it. They had shared tubs of ice-cream after broken relationships. Laughed and cried together; when Anna's Nana died, Rosie went to the funeral to support her best friend. Anna had taken Rosie to the hospital after she fell off her pushbike, cutting her knee open. Even though Anna laughed till she cried at the sight of the bike poking out of the high hedge, back wheel spinning at the time. They gave up bikes after that.

"Anna, I don't get 'given' anything. Everything I own is from charity shops, mostly. Knowing my luck, Dorothea Wodehouse was a miserly, miserable spinster and wants us to hear how her vast fortune has gone to a cat's home. I've probably been left a set of spoons or something. In any case, Mother and Dad have the same letter. If there's anything to inherit it will more than likely go to them. I didn't realise Dad had any relatives left on his side.

"It's exciting though, isn't it, Rosie? You can tell me all about it when you get back tomorrow. Has your mum invited you to dinner?"

"I expect Dad will persuade her. Which means something fishy, bland and covered in sauce."

"Well, do your best and then tell her you're not hungry. I was going to treat us to a takeout on your birthday. I'll bring it forward a few days. Pizza, Chinese or Indian?"

Before Rosie could answer, an awful commotion disturbed them from the small downstairs garden they shared. Bumble was chasing Bear and meowing loudly.

"Uh-oh, you better scoot, Rosie. I will see you in the morning. I've got to go shopping."

Rosie was already halfway down the stairs. Bear would come worse off if she didn't shoo Bumble away. Anna watched from the upstairs window, smiling, as her friend tried frantically to get muddy Bear out of a prickly rose bush. Dear Rosie. All freckles and red frizzy curls.

Anna was sure her friend's fridge was a little empty. It was the end of the month. She was writing down a few extras, hoping to slip them inside. Rosie was a proud lady and Anna wouldn't insult her. Anna knew the commission from her last two paintings would last her a good few weeks, it could be labelled 'early birthday treats' this time.

All about Dorothea

Rosie heard Bear's barking over the noise of the shower. It was only ten o'clock. Soon afterwards he stopped. Anna had a spare key and had let herself in. The pet sitter was running around deliberately, making the eight- month- old pup chase her. He loved that game! Rosie towel dried her hair and called out. "Be with you in a few minutes, Anna."

Anna was too busy playing with the noisy dog toy to answer. Rosie smiled and got dressed. Another note to self. New hair conditioner, it was going to take an age getting all the knots out of her long curly hair. She scooped up her clothes to put in the machine with the other washing. The powder had run out two days ago.

Still, her black tee-shirt and dark jeans didn't look as worn out as her grey whites.

"Morning, Anna. What have you got there?" Rosie just caught her friend closing the refrigerator.

"Birthday treats. Sit down, let me brush those knots out for you. By the way, you left your letter behind when you rushed downstairs yesterday. Here you are." Anna placed the letter on the worktop and held Rosie's hair with both hands, being careful not to pull it and having the decency not to mention a deep oil treatment.

"It isn't my birthday till next week and you already painted me the beautiful picture and you are buying..."

9

"Chinese tonight. Crispy duck? You do the same for me. Why I remember my last birthday. The beautiful flowers and the ..."

"Burgers. The flowers were from the garden."

"And lovely they were too. Don't forget you gave me the lovely porcelain vase."

"From the junk shop, Anna."

"Exactly so, much better than any old High Street rubbish." Anna gently teased the tangled knots out, while Rosie sat glancing around the kitchen. Washing up liquid. Tea bags. An uncut, fresh loaf from the bakery. A beautiful bunch of flowers propped in the kitchen bowl. Once again, Anna had bailed her out with essentials and treats. Bear ran around Rosie's legs, jumping up, not quite reaching her knees. Sitting in his small bed was a squeezy bone-shaped toy. It hadn't been there yesterday.

"I couldn't stop thinking about your visit today, Rosie. You must tell me all about your mysterious great aunt when you get home. Take as long as you like. Me and Bear are going to the park for a picnic lunch. He told me he likes a stroll on a lovely spring day."

"It's going to be a long wait till next Tuesday, Anna. The weekend weather should be fine. If I get paid early shall we pop out for a ride? I will put some petrol in the car. Bear likes to go exploring, it will give Bumble some peace."

"I'd already given that some thought. Nellie is full up and raring to go, she had her service this week and I thought we could go off for a picnic or something? Maybe a stroll along the seaside somewhere?"

"I'd like that, Anna. It's my weekend off. At least let me buy the chips and ice-cream!"

"Wouldn't have it any other way. Have you eaten? Don't want you having a nervous tummy today. We both know how Mildred aggravates your system." Rosie admitted she hadn't. Anna was right, her mother did upset her stomach.

True to form, Anna proved just what a great friend she was. Over the next hour, she blow-dried Rosie's hair, careful not to use a brush. The frizz turned into bouncy curls and all Rosie had to do was cuddle her cat and tuck into a delicious warm bacon baguette and two mugs of fresh tea. At 10.55 Rosie grabbed her bag, she was clean and full, ready to face her mother. She gave her dad, Walter, a warm peck on the cheek and got into his air-freshened and valeted Jaguar. Mother's choice of car. The woman was a self-centred snob.

"This is what my letter says, Dad. Is yours the same?" Rosie read out the formal wording, hoping to have most of their chatting done along the way.

"Pretty much, word for word if I'm not mistaken. I hadn't seen aunt Dorothea since I was about six years old. I really don't remember her. As you know, my father was killed in an accident and I only have a vague recollection of her at the funeral. All I know is she never got on with my mother much and I never saw her again. Mum told me before she passed away that Dorothea never married or had children. She was Dad's only sibling, his elder sister."

"So, she is an aunt you never really met then?"

"Correct. My grandparents on my father's side were rather well-off. They helped Mum when Dad died, paid off her mortgage and then the bungalow passed down to me. I think they left a large amount of money in their will to my mother who used it on my upbringing mostly. Then she passed what was left to me."

"So, Mother was rather lucky when she met you then. The bungalow was already signed over to you on condition Nan lived with us until she passed."

"Exactly. But I really can't tell you anything else about your 'Great Aunt Dorothea.' Of course, mother will deal with all of it, like she always does. But I do have a sizeable savings account of my own. My mother put it into trust for me. I've never needed most of it and I'm passing it over to you, Rosie. Next week, for your 25th birthday. Now then. I don't want to hear any word of protest and we will keep it between ourselves. Is that a deal?"

"Oh, Dad. I love you so much, thank you. But there isn't any need, really, I can manage."

"Nonsense, child. I can assure you there is a pretty penny in the account now. I've never done anything for you, I've never been allowed. And if it turns out Dorothea has left you nothing more than a tea-set, well, you won't be too disappointed. We shall meet in the town next week and sort out transferring the money over to you. Mother never need know." Walter Wodehouse smiled. He'd been waiting years to tell his daughter this, and now she only had days to wait.

"Is that you? I can smell animals all over you." Mildred Wodehouse stood with her hands on her hips, a waspy snarl curling her top lip. "Take your shoes off, Rose-A-Lyn. I've just had the carpets shampooed."

"Hello, Mother. It's nice to see you." The bungalow smelled of cod, or smoked haddock, or something similar. Rosie hung her big cloth bag on the coat rack and placed her shoes in the porch on the rack. Her dad waited outside patiently. Once Rosie entered the long hallway, he would dutifully do the same. Shoes off, slippers on. Rosie pulled her sock over her big toe. Damn, trust her to grab a pair with a hole in. She scrunched her big toe hiding the offensive digit.

"Wash your hands. Lunch will be ready at noon, sharp."

"Wonderful. What have we got?" Rosie sarcastically muttered, before she winked at her dad and side-tracked to the bathroom. Her hands were clean, apart from where Bear had licked her bacon fingers. She felt sorry for Dad. No wonder he loved to potter around in the garden or mess about in his shed and greenhouse.

"The garden looks lovely, Dad. Very probably the neatest lawn in the whole cul-de-sac."

"Thank you, dear!" Walter surveyed his handiwork through the kitchen patio doors. Mildred would not have the lawn any other way; it had to be precise stripes. It wasn't how his parents used to keep it. Gone were the wildflowers, small fishpond and higgledy piggledy paving stones. The garden was neat, full of clinical colours. Tallest plants at the back, neat rows of plants in front. Rose bushes took pride of place on the partially sunny side. Even the greenhouse was hidden behind a wooden divider.

Dinner was a morbid affair. No talking at the table and Rosie managed to hide most of the fish under her potatoes, squashing it together in a small pile and declaring herself well and truly full. The taste of the yummy baguette was still fresh in her mouth.

"It's no wonder you have spots. Dry hair, brittle nails, a plump chin and walk inwards. I expect you don't have time to cook proper meals, do you? What a waste. You've hardly eaten half your meal," Mildred Wodehouse complained.

As Rosie had only actually eaten two mouthfuls, she was pleased her ruse had worked.

"Clear away the plates, Walter. I've made a sherry trifle. It's on the sideboard there. Make yourself useful."

Rosie hated the extra thick pink custard as her mother well knew. It was a predictable move, designed to add more hostility at the dinner table.

"Not for me, Dad. Thank you all the same. You are right of course, Mum. All the sugar gives me an outbreak. Adds to my chin. I'll put the kettle on if that's alright. Maybe we can clear up afterwards, once we've read our letters." Rosie stood and left the table. It was all she could do mostly, walk away.

"I can't stay too long today. Anna can only look after Bear until two o'clock. She is going out with her Mum today. They have lunch, go shopping, trawl the charity shops and top it all off with cake for tea and then they catch up on each other's news over posh sandwiches."

Walter sat down with two bowls of stodgy trifle. He didn't like peaches. Never had. He would have loved strawberries, or raspberries, but he was denied the pleasure. Rosie caught his eye and gave him a big smile. She lifted his heart and was the only woman in his life he really cared about.

Nothing came out of the conversation really. Rosie's dad repeated everything he'd said earlier. Her mother, Mildred, was only intrigued to know if there was money involved. The solicitors hadn't revealed anything to her. So, they agreed to meet at the office in the town on Tuesday. Rosie was going to make her own way there. She was equally excited to be meeting her father on her birthday, Monday. Mildred had already explained it was hairdresser day for her and had given Rosie a card and present to take home with her. No good wishes were relayed. Whatever it was, Dad would have paid for it.

"Where shall I meet you on Monday, Dad?" Rosie asked in the car.

"I'm coming to your flat to pick you up, darling. Don't worry, I will find a space somewhere I'm sure. Mother's appointment is at ten o'clock. I will drop her off and come straight over. She is meeting her friend, Audrey, afterwards. Bring your I.D, passport, utility bills, that sort of thing. I know you have a bank account, but if we have one at the same branch it makes it easier and instant to transfer the money to you."

"But, what will you do for money? You will save enough for yourself, won't you?"

"I'm not giving you all of it! Not all at once. I will have enough for a rainy day and when I'm gone, the rest is going straight to you."

"I am very grateful, Dad. Whatever it is. Sometimes it's a little difficult at the end of every month. But I never wanted Mum to help me, it's too..."

"Draining. Yes, I know. My mother could see it too. Which is why she passed along the bulk of the family money down to me, without your mother knowing. I didn't want to ask every time I wanted tomato plants, or a new hedge cutter. I get everything I need when I have time to myself."

"I love you, Dad." Rosie leaned over and gave her father a big hug and kiss before stepping out of the car.

"I love you too. See you Monday then. Have a nice meal with Anna!"

"Dad, how did you know!" Rosie laughed and headed to her flat. She could see Anna and Bear curled up on the sofa, watching TV. Walter tooted his horn and drove off a happy man.

Bear began barking and didn't stop, even when he could see it was Rosie walking in. Bumble arched her back, stood up walked around in a circle and sat back down in the armchair.

"Honey, I'm home!" Rosie joked.

"Let me guess, fish and trifle?"

"Got it in one!"

"Would I also be right in thinking you made a hasty exit. It's barely two-thirty!"

"Also correct; you know me so well." Rosie placed the card and neatly wrapped package with bow on the coffee table. The smell gave away the contents. The perfume department had done the wrapping.

"Eau de pong?" Anna smiled.

"Three out of three. She knows it gives me a rash. Anyway, Anna. How about a glass of wine? I spotted it in the fridge earlier! I've got stuff to tell you and the next six bottles are on me."

Birthday's and secrets

Rosie and Anna had one of the best weekends they'd ever shared. Several glasses of wine over a fantastic Chinese takeaway. Followed by an early payday for Rosie, resulting in a weekend of outings, no work and lots of fun.

Anna was very happy for her friend. Whatever Walter was going to give her, which was a secret only the three of them would ever know about, was going to be a big help. Not only that, Rosie had this mysterious meeting on Tuesday afternoon and to top it all, Anna now had the oil painting of Bear and Bumble framed and ready to hang.

Rosie had been too proud for too long. Everyone needed a small amount of help now and again and as she wouldn't be struggling, she'd be able to have the odd night out with Anna, fill her bathroom cabinet and buy some well-needed clothes. Probably from the charity shops! Nothing else was on Rosie's radar.

A little before ten thirty Monday morning, Walter pulled up a few doors away and walked to the flat. He was whistling, chirpy and had a definite spring in his step!

"Good morning, Mr. Wodehouse," Anna called down. She'd collected Bear and was taking him to her place for a while this morning. There was no way she was going to intrude on father daughter time. Besides, she'd been downstairs since eight o'clock! This time with a thoughtful present. A natural fragrance, the only one Rosie really liked, and it didn't irritate her skin. Anna had it filled into an antique glass bottle with a dainty sprayer.

"Good morning, Anna. Lovely day!" Walter called up the stairs.

Rosie came charging out of her flat. "Ta-da!" She did a twirl. The birthday girl looked radiant in the second-hand washed clothes she had found on her travels over the weekend. She wore a long flowing dark floral skirt, a pretty, embroidered top and denim jacket. The floppy summer hat really made her freshly washed and conditioned locks stand out. She smelled of roses and lily of the valley.

"Look at you! Happy birthday, Rosie." The two embraced and after making sure she had everything she needed, they went off arm in arm for their secret morning out. Walter was dressed for the occasion too. He was wearing his best trousers, new shoes and a smart shirt. Not that his wife took much notice. Rosie smelled a dabble of Old Spice. Her dad had never changed his aftershave!

"Will we have time for a birthday lunch, Dad?" In all her innocence, Rosie had no real idea of how significant the bank meeting was going to be, it could take a little while.

"Yes. I've already booked a table for two. The meal is on you, sweetheart, you can treat your old Dad!"

Rosie laughed. "Of course, I will. I've just been paid." She certainly didn't take after her mother. Whatever her dad was going to give her would hopefully last till the end of the month and she could pay her bills, feed the pets and not worry for four weeks.

An hour later, Rosie's jaw almost dropped to the floor. In complete silence she looked at the balance in her new account and was lost for words.

"I didn't want her son getting any of it. Mildred's already leaving him her personal money in her will. So fair is fair. I will make sure the bungalow will eventually be passed down to you. My mother bequeathed it to me, with the request it's passed down to only you."

"Let's talk about everything over lunch, Dad." Rosie gave him a nudge on the foot. The bank clerk was waiting for a signature from Rosie and was far too interested in their private business.

~

Mildred Wodehouse had a two-year-old son when she met Walter. Something he didn't know about for a good few weeks. She'd chosen to drop that bombshell on him after he proposed, and their wedding date was set. The boy's father had scarpered. His family emigrated to Australia, soon after Mildred made the announcement; she was pregnant. It had always been the father's intention to go, his family just brought it forward a few months. Here today, gone tomorrow.

It turned out Mildred didn't even know his surname. Yes, her mother had a drunken fumble. Miss prim and proper wasn't so angelic. So, all in all, Mildred fell on her feet. Nana Wodehouse had done the right thing keeping her money a secret between her and Walter. She'd even gone so far as to tell her son he was gullible. "Walter, you have been well and truly used," were her precise words, even if hypocritical.

Rosie was not about to tell her father the same thing. That her mother had used him and thought more about her son than she ever had Rosie or him. In fact, Rosie and her dad went straight from the bank to his solicitor. That day, he made his last will and testament legally binding, superseding anything previously written. The deeds to the bungalow were in Dad's name. If he died before Mildred the house passed down to Rosie. She would allow Mildred to remain in the house for the rest of her life and then the property would be sold. All proceeds went to Rosie, no share to Michael Smith, son of

Mildred. Michael had taken his mother's surname at birth and it had never been changed to Walter's.

The other clauses included his wife could keep the assets in his joint account, but the remainder of the contents of his personal bank account were to go directly to his daughter, Rosie. Firstly, his funeral expenses were to be deducted. The papers were signed and witnessed by Walter, Rosie, the solicitor and his assistant. Walter also left the deeds to the bungalow in the possession of the solicitor. Everything was watertight. His mother's terms and his own were clearly written.

"Wow! I didn't expect my 25th birthday was going to be this formal, or how much it would change my life. Do you know what, Dad? I've never liked tele-sales. In fact, I'm not going back to it at all now."

"That's my girl. How do you fancy a steak? On you of course!"

"I think I have enough money now to buy steak dinners for the rest of my life. I feel like I've won the lottery."

"Well, you are old enough now to be sensible with it and I can't tell you how relieved I am to have it all sorted out."

"Why don't you just leave her?" Rosie spurted out over lunch.

"I'm sixty years old, Rosie. What would I do? Where would I go?"

"You'd come with me. If you can put up with Bear and Bumble of course! Who knows? Tomorrow is another day and we still must find out what this will is all about. Why not be a devil? Me and Anna are having a huge birthday cake tonight. Say you'll stay!"

"I can stay for the evening at least, why not? I'd love to! I really hope Dorothea has left me nothing more than a clapped-out lawnmower. If there's anything of any real value. I hope she's left it for you, Rosie."

Rosie's head was in a spin that evening. It was her turn to do the treating. Anna didn't refuse a few glasses of wine. Walter stuck to cups of tea. He had driving to do. Besides, he'd been naughty enough for one day, telling his wife he would stay out for as long as he jolly well liked!

He left at ten o'clock that evening after many hours spent laughing and joking. Oh, how he'd missed out over the years. That was all about to change. He'd worked out he had more than enough to take care of himself for the rest of his days. Rosie was set now, and the family bungalow would give her another small fortune one day.

There was more to Dorothea Wodehouse than anybody knew. For whatever reason his aunt hadn't liked Nana Wodehouse, nobody knew. But she had adored her brother and once she had found out Nana Wodehouse had passed on, she changed her will.

Her nephew, Walter and his daughter, Rosalyn, would benefit from her on her passing. Nothing was bequeathed to Mildred Wodehouse. Well, almost nothing. Dorothea had made it her business to find out all about her and her son, Michael.

No, they would not benefit at all. Walter Wodehouse and Rosalyn Wodehouse were the only beneficiaries. Dorothea had two things to leave. One to her nephew and one to her great niece. The child had been left out over the years, ridiculed by a spiteful mother. And Walter's happiness was long overdue.

At every given opportunity, Mildred had belittled Walter and shunned her daughter. Her son never took Walter as his own father nor his sister as someone he was close to. As soon as he was old enough to understand, Mildred had told her son they were lucky to have a roof and that hers and Walter's love affair had been very short-lived. She wished she only had one child. And it showed, every day.

Rosie had decided not to divulge anything on the evening of her birthday. Once again, Anna was pet sitting on the day of the will reading. It would be the last time for a while. Rosie had no immediate plans for work over the next month at least. She was taking a well-earned break. For nine solid years she had worked and for the last three just managing to make ends meet after she'd finally left home. She had only ever stuck around for so long to keep her dad company.

If yesterday was a memorable day it was going to be equally met by events this afternoon. Her mother hadn't rung yesterday to wish her a happy birthday. In fact, the only time she'd rung in months was to have a nose about the solicitor's letter.

"My stomach is doing somersaults, Anna," Rosie said, nervously.

"Take deep breaths my friend. You'll be fine. Listen, your taxi has just pulled up. Hurry go on - you don't want to be late. We'll be here waiting. I want to know all the details!"

Anna watched as Rosie walked up the path. Bear was barking and yapping, watching his mistress disappear through the gate.

The reading of the will

Arkwright & Sullivan's Solicitors, was in the town centre. Rosie jumped out of the taxi with ten minutes to spare. It felt good to give a little tip. She knew only too well what it was like to count pennies. The building oozed wealth. There was something about it screaming it had an upper-class clientele. Set back from the pathway were black glossed painted railings, tall plants in posh planters either side of the steps and a thick brass plaque with heavy black engraving.

Rosie pushed open the heavy door after pulling it the wrong way and stepped inside. Her parents sat in the reception area. Before the receptionist could speak, Rosie took the chair next to her father. Her mother gave her a frosty glare, no doubt spotting a few dog hairs on her dark trousers.

"Hi Mum, hi Dad. Sorry, I'm late. The traffic was terrible." They still had five minutes to go and the loud clock was the only sound in the silent office. Her mother ignored her.

"Don't worry, Rosie," her dad whispered. "We wouldn't have started without you." She felt his warm hand grab hers.

Mildred sat with the letter on her legs tapping her foot impatiently. Of course, she felt she needed to be controlling the whole proceedings. It was one-minute past two when they were called into the office of Mr. Arkwright Snr. His secretary showed them to their seats, offered tea or coffee and then left the room. Mildred took the chair opposite the solicitor and pulled herself forward.

Walter was surprised the will had actually been hand-written by Dorothea and it wasn't just a case of an office team finding any living relatives through public records. The reading began.

To Mrs. Mildred Elicia Wodehouse: I leave two fox fur stoles, a string of pearls and a box of linens.

To Mr. Walter Derek Wodehouse: I leave my gardening business based in Bromington-on-sea. Full details are enclosed for your perusal.

To Miss. Rosalyn Wodehouse: I leave the remainder of my estate. An establishment in Bromington-on-sea and adequate funds to renovate the property. Any surplus amounts will be divided equally between The Red Cross and Battersea Dog's home. Full details are enclosed for your perusal.

Terms and conditions apply.

Mildred stomped from the room, banging the door behind her, not bothering to listen to the rest. Walter apologised and he sat with Rosie while Mr. Arkwright Snr. explained everything in the small print. All of it seemed straightforward enough. Walter was free to keep the business providing he kept the staff who were currently employed under the temporary manager. There was a small cottage on site which went with the business for family use only. Walter could stay there for his natural life. After which, it could be passed down to his daughter, Rosalyn, and her family. Plus, any future spouse/s of Walter. It gave no mention of the wife he had now!

A copy of customer list and rates was all neatly hand-written as were all the gardening business documents inside a large black box.

Rosie and Walter were shown photos of the establishment, which was in fact a Bed and Breakfast. Currently it was closed and in a poor state of repair. It wasn't one building, but two, semi-detached and interconnecting. One building was set aside for the owner and the other had six rooms to be rented out on a nightly basis. The terms were, Rosie would run this place as her own following renovations and updating. On Rosie's death it would be passed down to a family member.

"What if I don't have a family?" Rosie asked.

"Then the terms state you will donate the buildings to a worthy successor," Mr. Arkwright Snr. explained.

"Hmm. Bromington-on-sea." Walter scratched his head.

"On the South-West coast, Mr. Wodehouse. Not too far from Devon. The gardening business is three miles away from the Bed and Breakfast."

"Where did Dorothea live?" Rosie asked.

"In a floor at the top of the establishment as she called it. For the last ten years it was all too much for her. She retired at 85 you know. Quite enough for most of us. For the last few years she lived alone with her pets and spent her days watching the sea."

"I wish I'd known her," Rosie sighed.

"Oh, perhaps you will! There are those who believe she hasn't left the building! The spirit of Dorothea lives on if tales are to be believed. She passed on six months ago, leaving instruction for the will to be opened today. It was important to her for some reason."

"It is the anniversary of my father's death," Walter said quietly. "Fifty-four years ago, today."

"And you lost contact with her?"

"Straight after my father's funeral, as far as I know. For some reason she didn't hit it off with my mother."

"Whatever her reasons for staying away, Mr. Wodehouse, she is making it up to you now. Very affluent area, Bromington. Would you both like to sign here to say you have received the following: Deeds, copies of the last will and testament, two sets of keys. A cheque in advance to begin renovation works.

Please have all builder's bills sent directly to me. My orders are not to disclose the monetary amount left in the will. Rest assured you don't need to scrimp. In fact, the places will need rewiring, new rooves and updating from top to bottom. When you are sure you have finished, the surplus will be divided equally for the charities."

"Silly question, but what if we refused to accept the offer?"

"Quite simply it all goes to charity, Mr. Wodehouse."

"Then, where do we sign?" Walter laughed. His wife could take it or leave it. He was going to Bromington-on-sea as soon as he could.

"Can I take my friend with me?" Rosie asked.

"Of course. This will be your house to do with as you please until you pass it on."

"So, if I ever have a family, it will belong to them to do as they please."

"Quite, Miss. Wodehouse."

Somewhere in the town, Mildred Wodehouse was stomping along, fuming. The solicitor's letter screwed up and tossed in a bin. The woman could take her pearls and shove them up her... where the sun didn't shine. If her husband thought, they were going to take over some gardening business he could think

26

again. They weren't going anywhere. She would see to it. When he got home, he could jolly well go outside and mow the lawn. The most humiliating thing now was having to tell her Michael.

She shouldn't have promised him they were going to be rich. In fact, all their plans they made the day before were now out of the window. Far from going to the hairdresser's, she had spent the day with her son. He was far more important to her than her daughter would ever be. Rose-a-lyn was, well, she had no class and was ginger, like her father. Michael was going places. Now it would just take him a little longer. Maybe he'd have to wait for Walter Wodehouse to pass away. At least then they'd sell the bungalow she secretly detested, take the proceeds and any money she always felt her husband hid from her.

In fact, Mildred was fuming. She walked into her local bank and opened herself a savings account. In her name only. Then she proceeded to transfer most of the money from hers and Walter's joint account. She left the bare bones to cover the month's bills. From now on she was taking the lion's share of his earnings as well, it was going in her savings. She felt slightly better after going for a coffee.

Walter was a fair man, not a vindictive one; he gave to those who gave to him and from now on he was going to treat them the same as they treated him too. Whatever his wife was or wasn't doing with their joint account behind his back wouldn't worry him. For he still had over £50,000 in his own account. The bungalow would not pass down to their son, who had treated him with contempt most of his life.

"Do you fancy going for a ride out down to Bromington-on-sea this weekend?" Walter asked, once they'd left the solicitor's office.

"Yes Dad, you bet. But we need to go for the whole weekend. If Anna would be an angel and..."

"Why don't you ask her mother to pet sit for the weekend? She is a lovely lady; I'm sure she won't mind. I know you'd love Anna to come too!"

"You're right, Dad! I haven't told Anna how much you gave me. I still can't believe it myself."

"I told you, Dad's side of the family were very well off. They paid the outstanding mortgage on the bungalow and saw Nana was looked after. She took what she needed during her lifetime and passed the rest to me. Now, I'm passing it on to you. You need it now, not when I'm dead! Besides, it was never going to your mother.

It is your business, Rosie, what you tell Anna. But I don't think it matters to her one tiny bit. She has stood by your side through thick and thin, as you have her. Why, I think the house would be big enough for you, for her, and even her mum! It must be three stories high and no doubt there will be a basement too."

"And the cottage at the gardening business will be plenty big enough for you. Why don't you take it and have a break at least?"

"I've already given it serious thought, Rosie. When your mother goes to her bedroom tonight, I'm going to pack two suitcases over the coming days and gather all my personal belongings. She goes out every Friday. I could always pack everything in the boot, leave a note saying I've gone off to look at the gardening business for the weekend and make my mind up once I get there."

"Yes, and if Jane agrees to look after Bear and Bumble me and Anna can follow you down in her car. Whatever happens, I must come back again, there's so much to sort out. Anyway, why don't you drop me off and leave all the paperwork with me. I have a copy of your will too and I can put it all together safely. The less Mother knows about any of this the better. I use the term *Mother* loosely!"

"You're right, Rosie. I have some things, papers, photos and such like I would like to sort out anyway. Hopefully she won't be home yet."

"You really are the worm that's turned Dad, let's go. I can't keep any of this from Anna any longer. I'm bursting!"

Rosie could see Bear running along the back of the sofa as she got out of the car with two heavy bags. Anna looked out of the window and waved to Walter. She shut Bear in before he jumped down and then opened the front door to help Rosie.

"Rosie boo-boo, your face is fit to burst, come on, I'm dying to know the big mystery. Tell me it's exciting."

"Oh, it's more than that, much more than that. And Anna, my best friend in all the world, I want you to share it with me!"

Bumble strode past the two friends; the buzz was too much for her. Banging through the cat flap the hoity toity moggy sat aloof on the fence post with her back to the kitchen. Bear was doing his bits and pieces, non-stop barking. "Hold on, Anna – I can't possibly begin to talk to you with all this racket!"

Anna grinned, and put the kettle on. She changed her mind and opened the bottle of champagne left over from Rosie's birthday. It didn't sound very much as if Rosie had been left just a canteen of cutlery. She hoped it was something special, her best friend deserved a break.

Bear came charging into the kitchen, barking, yapping and jumping up Rosie's legs, like he hadn't seen her for days. She scooped him up and gave him a big kiss. In return she had a face wash like no other. He was licking her nose, not at all bothered by her freckles, or deep red hair. Unlike her mother, who found her an embarrassment. Michael was blond, like Mildred once was. Nowadays it came out of a bottle.

"Oh Anna, you would have died. Mother pushed her way into the room first, pulled her chair up and practically blocked me and Dad out of the way. Anyway, the solicitor eventually got to the reading of the will. You will never guess what great aunt Dorothea left her?"

"No, but I know you're itching to tell me! A stuffed owl, perhaps?"

"No. Two fox fur stoles, a pearl necklace and a box of linens."

"You are joking!"

"Nope. Then he moved on to Dad and then me. At this point, Mother stomped out and banged the door!"

"Go on. The suspense is killing me, what did you get?"

"Grab the wine glasses, you need to be sitting down for this, Anna."

Decisions and pastures new

Rosie and Anna perched on the tatty sofa and Bear jumped up between them, laying on his back waiting for a belly rub. Rosie raised her glass, "Cheers, Anna. Now where shall I begin?" she teased.

"Go back to yesterday. How did the bank meeting go? Tell me all about your day with your dad. I want to know how your birthday went first, apart from our cake of course and lovely evening. Did you go somewhere nice?"

Rosie loved this about Anna. Her genuine nature. The most important thing to her was the time her friend spent with her father.

"Okay, well we had a lovely lunch, Dad had booked a table at the Steak Palace, a surprise!"

"Wow, now you're talking! Me and Mum have thought about going there, but it's too expensive!"

"Well, he booked the table, but it was my treat."

"Are you serious? It probably took up half your weeks wages. Rosie, you know your fridge will be bare before the month's out," Anna scolded.

"I haven't finished yet! Let me fire up my laptop. This is the first thing I want to show you. Dad said he wanted me to wait until my 25th birthday, so I would be old enough to deal with it. He never truly knew how much I, well, how much I…"

"Went without every month?" Anna finished.

"Yes. I didn't want to worry him. Besides, I thought Mother had all the money. I wasn't going to give her the satisfaction of lecturing me. The only one who ever got anything was Michael. He went to college, got a new car. I often wondered why Dad never spoke up or treated me the same way as Mother treated my half- brother. But now I know. Look at this, Anna."

Rosie turned her laptop around to show her best friend her bank balance.

Anna gulped her champagne, tipped Rosie's glass up making her down hers and then refilled the glasses.

"Rosie boo-boo. Does that say what I think it does? Two hundred thous..."

"Yep. It does! Drink up. There's more!"

"More? I can't take any more!" Anna ripped open Rosie's box of luxury chocolates. 'Love from, Jane X'

"Come and sit down here. Oh, and by the way. Do you think your mum would be an absolute angel and flat sit this weekend? You, me and Dad are going to Bromington-on-sea Friday morning."

By the end of the evening the two friends were very tipsy.

"Say that to me again, Rosie. This time pinch my arm. You want me to come and live in a three-storey, huge house by the seaside, one floor for you, one floor for me, one floor for you, one floor for me," Anna slurred.

"That's quite correct. A floor for you, one for me and one for you and one for me and one for Bear, one for Bumble, Jane can come too. One for you and one for me." The two of them nodded off on the threadbare rug underneath a crotched throw with one large cushion each under their heads. The chocolate box was empty. So were two and a half bottles of champers, little Bear snuggled between them. Sometime during the night Bumble walked straight over them and jumped up onto her favourite armchair.

Everything was set and Jane turned up bright and early Friday morning. She hugged Rosie warmly.

"I could hardly make out what Anna was saying on the phone the other night. Were you two rascals drunk?"

"Not at all. Oh Jane, it's so exciting! Let me get you a drink. Anna will be down in a minute." Rosie blurted out the whole story. Apart from exactly how much money she had, but Jane got the point!

"I'm so happy for you, really I am. Show me the picture of the house." Jane studied it for a few minutes. "I can tell just by looking at it from the outside it has a warm feeling.

"I'm being perfectly serious you know. I couldn't go anywhere without Anna. There is no way I'd want her to leave you. Your flat is a rental, isn't it?"

"You really do mean this, don't you, Rosie?"

"I certainly do! I thought Anna could be at the top of the house. The views will be marvellous for her painting. Then the level under that could be yours. I would take the bottom level opening out to the garden, for Bear and Bumble. The basement could be used for storage; stuff for the Bed & Breakfast next door. Please say you'll think about it, Jane. We can all help in the Bed & Breakfast and the revenue will cover the bills. All of us could do what we wanted for most of the day. Anna can paint. You have your crafts and I want to, well, don't laugh, but I have always wanted to be a Private Investigator. I can always hide my distinctive hair!"

"What about your parents, will they come too?" Rosie could tell Anna's mum was certainly giving it some serious thought.

"Dad has been given a gardening business with a cottage and staff. Just up the road. Keep it to yourself, but he has all his stuff packed in the back of his car. He might not come back. They've never been happy. All Mother truly cares about is her son. Dad was a provider and Michael, well, he's just a user."

Just then Anna came out of her flat, locked the door and bounded down the stairs with her weekend bag. "Hiya Mum. What do you think of all the news then?"

Jane laughed. "Why don't you both go and enjoy your long weekend away. Take plenty of pictures then come back and tell me all about it!"

Rosie gave her a hug. "We will, then you can tell me all about the style you'd like on your floor!"

Jane tickled little Bear behind his ears, his tongue stuck out from one side of his mouth and he was totally chilled, ga-ga, as they both watched from the window. Rosie and Anna were so excited, and Walter greeted them with a warm hug. Then he turned and gave Jane a wave and a wink. Was that a tee-shirt and jeans he was wearing?

Jane Rose was a little envious watching the happy crew go on their merry way. The house did look lovely and her own life was rather empty. She spent all her spare time crafting and then sold her goods online. They were unique and it just about enabled her to be self-sufficient, like her daughter. Of course, she also loved gardens and pottered about in a few elderly friends' small yards or roof gardens.

Jane was very nurturing, kind and caring. Bear didn't bark at all in her company. In fact, the snuggly little boy had fallen asleep in her arms. She laid him down on the sofa and pulled the crotched blanket over his back. It was one she made Rosie for Christmas. Anna got one too. Even Bumble followed her into the kitchen and came over for a bit of a fuss before she ate. Rosie had a new coffee machine and the smell was very tempting. Jane topped up her mug and made a fuss of the loudly purring cat.

Jane was fifty-eight and she'd been a widow since Anna was a young girl. One minute, Chris was laughing in the garden, then he collapsed. No-one knew he had an underlying heart problem; the attack was swift, fatal and he was gone. Jane was widowed at age thirty-six. Her husband deceased at thirty-eight.

Life had not been easy, and her mum had been there to pick up the pieces and walk along with her daughter and granddaughter. As a child, Jane was lucky to have such well-travelled parents. Not only did Anna have a flat full of exotic foreign rugs, knick-knacks and figurines, Jane did too. They were close and then three became two.

Sipping her delicious coffee, Jane had found she'd wandered back into the lounge and was sitting in the fireside chair. Bumble was comfortably curled on her lap. She didn't mind sharing with her at all. Although Rosie never had anything luxurious, she had inside warmth and generosity flowing through her veins. Now the buzz of excitement was sending Jane into a dreamy like state, closing her eyes, she could imagine how it would be.

Three different personalities injecting life into a house crying out to be a home. The bones of Dorothea Wodehouse encouraging everyone around her to succeed. She didn't seem a bad old stick at all. Jane couldn't help but wonder why she'd taken such a dislike to Walter's mother after her brother died in an accident.

By all accounts, the lady had looked after her son and brought him up as best she could. The money given to her she hadn't squandered, instead, passing it down to Walter, who in turn had passed it down to his daughter. At least a lump sum of it. None of this was Jane's business. She was just glad to see the young woman so happy at last. Both Jane and Anna had helped her in very small doses when they could. Nothing obvious, for Rosie had too much pride. She was an astute young lady. Private Investigator, hey? Jane smiled.

Bumble was extremely comfy, and Jane didn't mind at all that she was leaving plenty of black and ginger hairs all over her dress. Just like her daughter she had pure black hair, only hers had two or three pieces of grey. Not much, just enough to prove she was a lady of a certain age which wasn't betrayed by her youthful, wrinkle free face. She had a few laughter lines and deep brown eyes. Her wedding ring remained on her finger. She'd never taken it off. White gold, it looked like silver, which was her choice of jewellery. Jane had the appearance of a gypsy crossed with a '60s hippy. This was her style.

The more she thought about it, the better of an idea it seemed. Neither her nor her daughter were materialistic. Both lived in rented flats. Apart from her chairs, bed and large wooden ottoman imported from Singapore, Jane mainly had throws, rugs, covers, ornaments. A move wouldn't be that much of an upheaval. She could always come back and visit her elderly friends a couple of times a year.

Still, enough now. She must not get too enthusiastic; it might not happen!

A fleeting thought shot through her mind. Walter didn't look the same today. Without the trappings of his overpowering wife he shone in his own right. His new hairstyle suited him too!

"We had a great chat this morning, Anna. Jane loved the photo of the houses. She liked the vibe!"

Anna laughed. "That's a good start then. If Mum's getting a positive feeling just by looking at a photo, it's a good omen. Do you know she's hardly ever wrong; her intuition is spot on, Rosie."

"She is very... how would you put it?"

"Sensitive."

"Yes, good word. Tuned in. Do you think she would know if the ghost of Dorothea roams the house?"

"Oh, without a doubt. Or anyone else for that matter. If we have a ghost, she will feel it before we even get to the front door!"

"I've been thinking about something else, Anna. Do you think it would be daft of me to want to be a sort of... investigator?"

"No. Not really! It beats tele-sales any day of the week. You might not have gone to college like your half-brother, but you've always had a very good brain, Rosie. Look how quickly you sort out crossword puzzles, or sums, or just general problems. You are quick thinking. I bet you have a high IQ score."

"You think?"

"I know."

"Did you notice Dad's new haircut? I think he's paid a visit to some hip and trendy barber's by mistake!"

"Suits him, Rosie. Your dad is a very handsome man in an oldie sort of way! I've never seen him wear trainers before. Nor a tee-shirt or jeans."

"Do you think he's having a mid-life crisis, Anna?"

"No. He's far too old for one of them, but don't tell him I said that. Maybe he's just unleashing the beast!"

"Hardly a lion. He's always been meek. It's what makes him who he is; I'm loving his new sense of defiance though. I'd like to see him happy."

"If we do all move, Rosie, and your dad too, won't you miss your Mother?"

Rosie had a moments reflection. "No."

Bromington

Walter was singing along to Radio Two. He had a lovely voice but was never allowed to use it. They were poodling along, and had arranged a stop off halfway there, before they set off earlier. It was probably more than a four-hour drive. Who cares if it took five? Mildred had never been one for family holidays. She had taken Michael on a few occasions, for a week by the sea, with the excuse Rosie would be better off staying at home. She didn't want two arguing children on her hands for a week.

Anna wasn't too far behind with Rosie. Walter made sure to keep them both in his rear-view mirror. He'd been careful to slip the note on the hall table as he and Mildred had left the bungalow earlier. She'd find it when she got the bus home. Her days out with Audrey were becoming more frequent. Not being totally brave, Walter had written...

Rosie called when I got home, suggesting it might be a good weekend for us to pop and see Dorothea's gardening business and establishment. I wasn't sure what time you'd be home, so we have made our way down there. Should be home by Sunday tea-time.

Walter.

That's if he ever went home at all. He'd told his regular gardening customers he was taking a month off, due to a family bereavement. The smaller jobs were being covered by young Justin. Walter had taken him on a couple of years ago. He could very well find himself the new business owner if Walter stayed in Bromington.

Mildred had enough in the bank to get by, and if she didn't, well, for the first time in her married life she would have to go to work. Everything that was of any value to him was in the boot of the car. And at this moment, sitting in the car behind him, his Rosie. He turned the volume up and crooned along to 'My Way' by Frank Sinatra. He'd never had so much fun! It was also nice not to see a scowling face sitting on his left-hand side continually moaning about anything and everything whilst taking every opportunity to remind him of his many shortcomings. The journey flew by and they all stopped halfway.

"Look Dad. It's just the same as the phone you have now. Only this one you top-up. There's nothing confusing and it's even got a proper keypad. I charged it up last night and it's ready to go, keep it in your car. I've put my number, Anna's, and Jane's in your contacts. And we all have your new number. You know you can answer it in peace, or text and you won't be spied on!"

"Rosie, it's brilliant. Thank you. I'm going to keep this one for all the new Bromington contacts. In fact, I might add a few more contacts and let the battery run out on my other phone. How's your chicken?"

"Lovely! Juicy. I'm not used to all this posh living!"

"This risotto is gorgeous. Thanks, Walter, my treat next time," Anna smiled. She meant it too. The fact Rosie was now minted hadn't changed the status quo.

"And my minted lamb shank makes a lovely change! In fact, the only fish I will eat from now on will be battered." They all laughed at Walter's quip.

After a filling lunch, the three set off again. In two hours, they would approach Bromington, which was roughly, tucked away somewhere between Somerset and Devon. A tiny seaside village which didn't attract too many touristy types, and very probably why 'Great Aunt Dorothea' preferred it. From their short amount of research, they had found both of their locations were tucked back away from the seafront, although it was visible from the top of the establishment. They were close to an area of outstanding beauty and several rivers. Walter was looking forward to going fishing in peace on his days off.

Two hours later they had reached their destination. They'd decided to visit the gardening business first and it wasn't what Walter was expecting at all! Green fingers must run in his family.

Pulling up in the large gravelled car park all three were glad to get out and stretch their legs! You couldn't miss the front. *D. Wodehouse* was proudly displayed on the garden centres small fruit and vegetable shop. Behind that were large white tunnels, full of plants. A small strawberry field and apple orchard enveloped a barn, workshop, restaurant and stone building, which could only be the accommodation. A few staff pottered around the place and Walter knew this was only part of the set-up.

The business had local contracts with the schools and council. Private residents also used their services. It was a much bigger business than Walter had at home. Which mainly consisted of cutting grass and hedges for the elderly. A bit of pruning and weeding, that type of thing.

Much to Walter's delight, he found a small river ran around the side of the field and beyond, surrounded by grassy banks and trees full of pink blossom. It was plenty wide enough for the small boat moored outside the stone building. Walter could easily see himself living here. No trouble!

An elderly gent made his way over to them. "Can I help you folk at all?" he asked, wiping his greasy hands with an old cloth.

"Good afternoon. I'm Walter, Walter Wodehouse. This is my daughter, Rosie, and her friend, Anna."

"Ah, Mr Wodehouse you say. A relative of Dorothea's, the one our solicitor told us to expect. Pleased to meet you. I'm Derek and I run the maintenance shop here. Excuse the state of me, I'm servicing one of the sit-on mowers. My wife runs the small café here. She always has home-made scones and a pot of tea on the go! Can't beat a good Devon tea, come and meet her!"

Sybil was lovely. Round and rosy-cheeked. With her big blonde curls everything about her was warm, friendly and bouncy.

"How do you do, Walter. We've been expecting you; we just didn't know when! Pleased to meet you, ladies. Sit yourselves down and have a warm drink. I'll show you around Riverside Cottage shortly. We don't live too far away, just up the road a bit."

Sybil spent a good half hour chatting with them before finally closing for half an hour.

The inside of the cottage was adorable. It hadn't been lived in for some time, although Sybil kept it clean and tidy on a weekly basis. The hearth was swept and there was a basket of logs sitting in it, all ready for the chilly nights when they came around again.

A small cottage suite with a fireside rocking chair filled the cosy room. A red and blue deep rug sat underneath an oblong walnut coffee table. The deep stone windowsills housed knick-knacks and a grandfather clock stood in the corner. There was a small TV, not obtrusive and a telephone.

The kitchen had a stable door and the view from the window was the riverside. A family sized table and dining chairs sat at one end. A large Aga stove in an alcove was in the opposite wall. A huge pantry and small utility come cloakroom completed the downstairs of the cottage. Upstairs was a large double room overlooking the river once more, two singles and a bathroom. Each was simply furnished, but with antique furniture. The new mattresses were still covered in plastic and the pillows, sheets and blankets were newly washed and pressed inside the ottomans.

Sitting on a chair in the smallest bedroom was a plastic bag full of old linens. Two fox fur stoles hung on the back. The small box on the windowsill no doubt had a string of pearls sitting inside.

"Well. I will leave you to have a look around by yourselves, Mr Wodehouse. I'm afraid you will have to go to the village stores to stock up with supplies. We weren't expecting you, see!"

"Dad! I know what I think - and I can see it in your eyes that you love it!"

"Come and give your dad a hug. I'm all welled up inside," Walter said, through eyes a little teary and with a frog in his throat.

"Tell you what, shall we all go and look at the establishment, go shopping and then all come back here? I don't think we'll be able to stay at the B and B for a few weeks, not while it's going to be renovated.

"Great idea, Rosie," Anna agreed. "But you can have the room with the gross furs."

"Perfect. I'll check the bulbs before we head off. You girls go downstairs, see what we need. I'll be down in a minute or two."

Walter sat on the edge of the bed. It was very comfortable. Then he tried it for size. King size. Much bigger than the single bed he slept alone in at the bungalow. Staring at the ceiling for a few moments, he tried to grab the feel of the place. Comfortable, that's what it was. Cosy, charming and... he wasn't going home. Nor did he want Mildred anywhere near it. Her vitriol was enough to turn every pot of Devon cream sour. When they came back from the village he was unpacking and here he would stay.

The view from the back-bedroom window was lovely. He followed the meandering river as far as the eye could see. How much of the land belonged to the business he wondered? The bathroom was also at the back of the house. The single bedrooms overlooked the shop and the roadside.

"It isn't quite empty in the pantry, Dad! Sybil has a store of home-made jams, marmalades and pickles, all with the shop name on. Seems the gardening business is a bit more than that!" Rosie shouted, from the bottom of the stairs.

They spent a good while searching through cupboards, drawers, in the small garden shed directly outside the cottage. Rosie noticed there was a small section fenced off with a whirly-gig and garden chairs. Perfect for when Bear came to visit! They could shut him in without worrying. The business was close to the 'B' road and river.

"We have a shopping list. Let's go and see the B & B!" Rosie beamed. She was excited, as was Anna.

Wodehouse Bed and Breakfast

About three miles along the road they spotted a sign, just. The hedgerow had almost covered it over. 'Wodehouse B & B'. On the right-hand side was a large stone house. When they slowed down, they could see it was the 'establishment'. One gateway led to the building, they drove past and turned into the gravel driveway around the back of the property which was large enough for several cars.

Like so many properties in the area, it was built from grey stone. The front had a low surrounding stone wall and many bushes and trees covered a lot of the windows. The back of the property had a high stone wall. Rosie could get a good idea of the garden size. It would be plenty big enough for Bear to explore. The only concern she had was Bumble being close to a road. But it was the same where she lived already. A gruff man came over to greet them.

"I'm Nigel, security. Don't mind me. Ian is the other guard we are working around the clock, keeping an eye on the place till you take over. Lock up when you go, we just stay outside in our vans keeping an eye." Walter walked off with him, asking a few questions.

"Are you dying to go inside?" Anna grabbed her friend's arm. "I love it already, even if it is a bit run down. Nothing that can't be fixed, Rosie!"

"Exactly, and remember, Dorothea has left ample funds to do it all up. We need to cut the trees back a bit. I think it's going to be pretty dark inside."

"I noticed a walkway on the other side of the road. I think it goes towards the village and the sea."

"Exactly, Anna. I know it's not that far away. Between the pine from the trees I can smell the sea air in the distance."

A dark shadow passed across the top front window. Nobody saw it and a moment later it happened again, just as the trio were about to enter the house. Once they reached the front door, they found there were two doors. The one to the right had a wooden sign hanging on two chains. 'Wodehouse B & B' The one to the left simply stated, 'Private Residence' They would find an interconnecting door in the hallway. Locked and bolted from the private side.

Luckily, it was still daylight. They soon found there was no electric connection as the house had stood empty for months. The musty smell indicated a lack of visitors too. A pile of letters lay on the floor behind the door. Rosie scooped them up and placed them on the table. Unlike the gardening business, the establishment didn't look like a duster had been used for months! The house was huge! Every floor had plumbing and either a shower or bathroom. Although there was only one kitchen on the ground floor.

The girls were right. A ground, first and second floor, plus a basement and cellar. The good news was, Walter hadn't found any damp areas. Although the second floor had a few wet patches in the corners. Nothing that couldn't be fixed with the new roof.

Everywhere had wooden floors which were going to look stunning after a bit of work. The high ceilings had ornate centre roses and chandeliers. All had original fireplaces. The light fittings and plug sockets were very dated.

Rosie was taking pictures as promised, so too was Anna. Jane would love browsing through them tonight. Although none of them had anywhere near enough furniture to fill the spaces! It was going to be very easy to adjust the place into three separate dwellings with the main stairwell leading up and a main side door going out into the private garden for all to use. A six-foot fence separated their garden from the one belonging to the B & B.

Of course, the Bed & Breakfast side was already split into six rooms, all with en-suite. Downstairs had a large dining room, kitchen and a front room with sofas and leaflets for local attractions. Like the residential half, it needed a good rewire, new roof, update of all bathrooms and general decoration.

"I love it, Rosie. With a bit of light, the upstairs will be perfect for my portraits. The space is huge! I know Mum is going to be blown away too. What do you think?"

"It feels like home. There's no way one week ago when I was struggling to feed myself, did I think a few days later…"

"You would be a wealthy young woman, living in a drop-dead gorgeous property with your favourite ladies for company…"

Walter had his back to them. The part about Rosie struggling for food was too much to bear. Oh, god. He had some making up to do; not once had she grumbled or complained. How many times had Anna bailed his daughter out he wondered?

"Let's drive down to the village ladies, they might have strict opening hours around these parts!" Walter was going to get plenty of treats for the weekend. They didn't have far to go and found the perfect place with cobbled paving and free parking for thirty minutes.

"What do we have here then?" Rosie wondered. A teashop, naturally. Bakers, butchers, newsagents, unisex hairdressers, gift shop, a library, two pubs, a corner shop and pet store. There appeared to be a church on a hill and a village hall, which had regular jumble sales according to the notice in the newsagent's window.

A few fishing boats and private boats were moored further along in a small harbour. The tide was out and Anna was enthusiastically snapping photographs from every angle.

"Bear will love the beach, Dad. I think it's less than a ten-minute walk from the B & B." They all toddled off for a while.

"I think I will raise a glass to great aunt Dorothea this evening. I found some of my favourite bitter in the newsagents. There's an off-licence in the back. I've got plenty of bits for a hearty breakfast." Walter was more than happy.

"And I have freshly baked bread, scones and cream, butter, cheese, ham and milk!" Anna had two bags full.

"I've been busy nosing at the local adverts. I've grabbed a newspaper, fresh juice, bottles of wine and light bulbs, just in case. Oh, teabags, coffee and sugar too. Anyone fancy a cornet? Cornish, yum."

Walter and Anna put all the shopping in the boot of her car. His was full, but not for much longer. It would all be unpacked this evening.

The three of them sat on a bench gazing out to sea. They were enjoying the best ice-cream they ever had. A group of people were having a good look at them. Dorothea's name hadn't gone un-noticed. Not everyone in these parts would welcome her relatives with open arms.

"So, the rumours are true then. She did have relatives after all."

"It would seem, that way, yes. Now we have to work out how to get them out of the way."

"Leave it with me. I did think after all these months we were in with a chance."

"Yes, as soon as the security men left, but it might mean they are moving straight in, then what?"

The two men and two women carried on walking towards the harbour. Anna unintentionally took a photo of them from behind. She was catching the red sun over the waves.

"It'll be getting dusky soon. We better get back," Walter wiped his mouth and walked to his car.

Everything was closed when they got back to the garden business. But it seemed Sybil had spent a little time settling them in before she left. The curtains were closed but the lamps had been left on upstairs and downstairs.

A fragrant vase of fresh flowers was overflowing atop the dining table and a welcome card rested beside them, from Sybil, Derek and the staff. There was a smell of polish and air freshener. It was a lovely surprise to find all three beds made up with clean linen. None of your duvets! They had crisp white sheets, blankets and candlewick bedspreads. Fresh towels had been placed on the beds and guest toiletries were placed in the bathroom. Walter put his cases on the bed and began hanging his suits, shirts, trousers, cardigans and jumpers inside the double wardrobe. He had a few pairs of new jeans and tee-shirts and sat pulling the labels off. After placing his socks and underwear in the drawers he hung his dressing-gown on the hook at the back of the door. He put his pyjamas on the pillow.

He slid the two cases underneath the bed and put his toothbrush, paste and shaving kit in the cabinet. One end of the bathroom had a walk-in shower and there was a deep large bathtub at the other. One toilet upstairs and a downstairs cloakroom. He'd have plenty of room for guests, the cottage was far too big for him! Last, but not least, he put his hairbrush, gel and after-shave on the dresser top. Which had three old-fashioned embroidered doilies. He placed his reading book and glasses on the small bedside locker with the Victorian reading lamp. He'd noticed security lighting came on as they drove in, which wasn't a bad thing when you were out in the sticks. Maybe he should get a dog too?

The young ladies didn't take any time at all putting away their weekend stuff. Sybil had also taken the liberty of removing the items from the small bedroom. She had placed them in a downstairs cupboard instead. There didn't seem to be any Mildred Wodehouse on this trip. Come to think of it, Mr. Wodehouse hadn't even mentioned her. Still, it was none of their business. Derek and Sybil Hawkins knew how to mind their own!

Walter found a jug of milk in the fridge which Sybil had probably brought over from the small garden café and two clean tea-towels left on the drainer. A little basket housed a few teabags and coffee sachets. This lady had done more for him in the last hour or two than his wife ever had. He locked and bolted the front door and the three of them sat out in the garden for a while. Security lights lit the patio area and they laughed and joked over a few drinks. Walter hadn't actually enjoyed a pint since Christmas. That wasn't at home!

A large car slowed down as it went past the 'Garden Centre' as it was known around these parts. So, this is where they all were; the same place as the pearls. They would form a plan, after all, they'd waited far too long. The car sped off. They must be alert, ready to pounce. Duncan and Ivan were racking their brains for an answer. Damn Dorothea Wodehouse, this was all her fault. Perhaps burglary was the best option now.

"You're not going back again, are you?" Rosie eventually asked.

"No. Do you blame me? Look at this place, and the people. I'm in love with it already! I would feel a little happier if I put gates on the front though, just to secure it at night. Everything here is a bit open."

"I thought the same, if I'm honest. Perhaps the B & B should have outside security lights too, Rosie? The country is a bit, well... dark, isn't it?" Anna laughed, then they all did. It certainly was. There were no streetlights here.

It had been a long day and by eleven o'clock they were all tucked up in their rooms. Each of them dreaming about pastures new and the decisions they'd made. This really was an all or nothing situation, they were going to need each other in a small place like this.

Back in London, Jane had pulled out the sofa bed and was flitting between watching an old movie, tickling Bear and scrolling through the photos on her mobile. She stretched them out for a better view. It was a yes from her as well; the others had whooped with delight as they'd raised their glasses in the riverside garden earlier. Bumble sauntered out of the room and banged the cat-flap, she wouldn't be back for a few hours.

Maybe she was getting tired, but Jane would swear she could see a face looking out of the top window of the house. In the Bed & Breakfast half. The harbour and seafront was lovely, but something about the strangers in the distance made her shiver. Goosebumps spread over her arms.

The phone dropped from her hand ten minutes later, her tired eyes closed, and she fell asleep dreaming of her possible new life.

Back at the bungalow, Mildred hadn't even noticed her husband was missing for most of the evening. Having arrived home at tea-time and plonking her handbag in the hallway, right on top of his note, she'd headed for the bathroom. After spending the day with Michael, she had quite a headache. Mildred swallowed two painkillers and had a long soak in the bath. She painted her nails, admired her new bank account balance, flounced around in her new dressing-gown and slippers and finally realised Walter was not at home. Remembering where her bag was, she switched on the hall light to retrieve her phone. Then she spotted the note. Furiously she dialled his number. How dare they both go off like that.

Hadn't she told him plain enough, there was no way they were going anywhere. Running some place for a miserable old hag they'd never met. It wasn't as if they'd get anything for their troubles at the end of it. If his daughter wanted to go and live in some broken down place let her get on with it.

Those words were the only ones Walter had taken in at the time. *His* daughter? Later that evening he'd packed everything, including the few photos of Rosie growing up.

'You've reached the voicemail of Walter Wodehouse Gardening Services. I'm afraid I'm unavailable right now, please contact the office number instead...' "How dare you! Who do you think you are, going off like that? You and your daughter. Don't worry about me left here all on my own, will you. What do you think you're playing at? Sunday? Sunday?" she screeched. "You better be back in this bungalow by tomorrow, Wal-ter Wodehouse."

Walter deleted the voicemail when he slid into his kingsize bed, he switched the phone off and removed the battery. *No more, Mildred; enough is enough.*

There and back again

Rosie had decided, as did Anna, on a plan. Jane was on board as well. The three of them were going to work as a team. The girls hired a van for two weeks. Rosie had no furniture worth keeping, it was all being collected by the charity shops. She had taken her personal items from the flat, along with Anna's and they were being transported bit by bit over to her dad's new place; temporarily. It was all happening!

His dining room was home to several boxes. As soon as Sybil saw Anna's wonderful painting's she suggested they all be hung on the café walls. 'By local artist' they said, sporting various price tags. There was a lot of footfall in the Garden Centre every week. This could also possibly be a good place for Jane to temporarily sell her wares at one end. Sybil had a feeling the bag of linens would go to better use if Jane took them. The two women had only met once but took an instant liking to each other.

Meanwhile, Bear was under Jane's wing, out of the way at her place, while Rosie and Anna spent their days supervising work at the B & B. Jane decided not to move Bumble. Cat's didn't like change. She spent an hour or so with her every day while she fed her.

Mildred was determined not to take any of this lying down. After no communication from her husband in two weeks, she was making her own way down to Bromington-on-sea. Well, almost. Her son was going with her. Only they weren't going to make their visit known. Her only intention was to ruin whatever it was that was going on. She also realised she had no money coming in with her husband away. He'd be more valuable dead. They had arranged to make the journey one week from now if Walter had not made contact. Even Mildred realised he had taken everything. The bathroom cabinet was empty. All his clothes were gone. Twice she had gone to her daughters flat, the blinds were drawn. No-one was home, and neither did the girl answer her phone.

Walter was on the way to have the pearl necklace appraised. Somehow, he didn't think anything belonging to Dorothea would be cheap. Although, he would be surprised if they were anything of the nature of South Sea pearls. After all, the will hadn't been specific, nor had it mentioned the fact the pearls were a double strand. The vintage fox furs had a value of around £300 each. They were already boxed and ready to post. Quite rightly, everyone agreed they were offensive. Apparently, Dorothea was an animal lover and it was quite out of character for her to have something like this.

"Probably full of fleas too." Sybil had complained. The linens were beautiful. Very probably French vintage. Sybil loved the collection, as did Jane, who truly appreciated fabrics. Which got the café manager to thinking: This Mildred still hadn't made an appearance and there was plenty of old toot from jumble sales hanging around at home...

By lunchtime, Mildred's large package was all ready to be shipped to the bungalow. The single string of pearls, the cheapest Walter could find, were not the same as the set he'd sold earlier. His wife had made her decision in the solicitors office, she wanted no part of this new life. Her hatred for him and Rosie had quickly escalated that day. It was obvious, all she wanted was money, she didn't care about anyone except herself and Michael. Her only goal was how much she could extract from Walter. He'd been a fool for far too many years.

The large B & B building works were well under way. Scaffolding surrounded the stonework as soon as the tree fellers had finished. Two large trees had been cut right back, exposing the windows and some had been cleared away altogether. Walter was in his element, clearing the back gardens of debris, planting colourful wildflowers and putting together a rockery.

"This trunk is so heavy, Anna. We'll have to get some of the workers to clear this loft out for us. They can take everything down to the basement."

"Lock it up and keep the key safe, Rosie. I'm sure when you have time you might want to go through all of your Great Aunt's personal stuff."

"You bet. I don't know anything about her, why did she fall out with Nana? How did she know about me? Come to that, she specifically left Mother out of any of this, apart from a few bits."

"Perhaps she's been watching you from afar! I wonder what she'd think about me and Mum living here too?"

"Well, if she does know anything about me at all, Anna, then she would know only too well how you've helped me over the last three years. The extra bits in my fridge didn't just jump in there you know! And don't think I didn't spot how my electric meter went from £3 to £23 and things like that. Not that I'm not grateful, it's just that..."

"Oh, stop it. My meter was topped up too! Mum helped both of us sometimes; there's only so long a girl can live from selling paintings you know!"

"You are so lucky, Anna. Jane is lovely. I wish I'd had..." Rosie stopped talking. "Oh, I miss Bear, and Bumble."

"Look at this, Mum sent a short video this morning. I forgot!"

Rosie laughed at Bear's antics. He was rolling on his back for a tummy rub. Every time Jane stopped tickling him, he barked for more. A dark shadow passed over the screen. Instinctively they both looked to the window, but nothing was there. Rosie couldn't help feeling she would be put to the test once they'd settled in. She wasn't a sensitive, like Jane, but even she felt a presence, and the urgency to do a bit of digging. And not the kind her dad was doing most days.

Sybil banged on the Private Residence door, Anna let her in. "Do you fancy coming up to the jumble sale this afternoon, ladies? You never know what you might find for this B & B of yours!" Sybil was doing her daily rounds in the small Garden Centre van. Betty, Sybil's sister, was working in the café today. "Besides, I can introduce you to some of the locals if you like. The place is buzzing you know, you haven't really got to know anyone yet. They won't be happy till they know everything about you!"

"Sounds great. We'd love to," Rosie chirped.

It was Saturday morning and Walter was at the Garden Centre, supervising the installation of two large sturdy gates. Work had begun three days ago. Wooden fencing now adjoined the stone wall surrounding the centre, complete with fence spikes. A security system was in place and CCTV; discreetly placed high in trees both sides. The two gates had an intercom and were remotely operated. The Centre was closing at 3p.m. today, earlier than usual and Walter would have the gates open by 7.30 a.m. each day for the staff until 6 p.m. when the last of them went home.

By this evening he would feel a lot less vulnerable and all thoughts of a guard dog had now reduced to something along the lines of a Westie! A friendly companion was all he really wanted.

"I've been saying it for years, Walter. The place has been far too open. Too easy for anyone to break in to. We've only ever had an alarm on the café a dodgy camera and heavy padlocks everywhere else."

"It'll be like Fort Knox from now on, Derek. And by the way, if you ever see this woman come a knocking, make out you and Sybil live in Riverside Cottage. Tell her the employer accommodation is a pullout bed at the back of the café, in the store-room!" Walter passed over a photo from his wallet.

Derek burst out laughing. "Is this your lady wife?"

"Was. Not anymore. I've wasted too many years of my life as it is. I packed her parcel up during the week and Sybil posted it down to her. Nope, if she wants looking after from now on, she can get that son of hers to do her bidding. I don't even want to see her again. Keep the photo, make sure Sybil and the staff are aware. I have a feeling sooner or later she will be down here, causing trouble. First thing Monday I'm off to see about getting a divorce."

Walter patted Derek on the back. "Don't worry, Walter. You'll be safe with us."

Indeed, Mildred had received her parcel on Wednesday that week. Two moth-eaten pieces of fur, a pile of stained, pressed serviettes and tablecloths, courtesy of Sybil, and a green box with a string of pearls, which were the only things that didn't go straight in the bin. A string of freshwater pearls worth under £50. Mildred's greedy eyes had opened wide. But, her and Michael had bigger fish to fry.

"Michael. I've told you. He's gone. That daughter of his has gone too. I've searched high and low. I can't find the deeds anywhere. How can I sell the bungalow without them? I need to get some legal advice. Don't worry. If he has anything of any value at Bromington-on-sea I will be claiming my half of that too."

"Do you have life insurance?"

"Of course we do. All of it is paid up as well. Why do you ask?"

"What if he never comes back? Have you thought about that? The bungalow is in his name, you said so often enough. He might sell it and then where will you be?"

"I'm sure he would never dare do that, besides, half of it belongs to me, by law."

"Are you sure? He seems to be in pretty thick with Rosie, you didn't see that coming, did you? The bungalow may have her name on the deeds for all you know."

"I wish I'd never laid eyes on that child. It wasn't my intention to fall pregnant with her. Somehow it committed him to me. I made sure it never happened again."

"Yes, Mother I know. He has spent the entirety of your marriage sleeping in the small bedroom."

"Where else could I put him? You had the other double room, naturally, then your sister needed a room. It was all that was left for him."

In fact, Michael was spot on with his earlier remark. Walter and Rosie had consulted with his solicitor and the conveyancing team again and alterations had been made. The deeds were in Rosie's name now. They were also in her possession. All legal and above board, she was the new owner of the bungalow, it had been transferred over to her. But both had agreed, Mother could live there for the rest of her days. Walter wouldn't see her homeless. It was a family home, Mother had never worked or contributed to it in any financial way. It was Walter's alone to do with as he pleased, and he had. And it pleased him very much.

Michael Smith. Almost twenty-eight. Blond. A bachelor. He graduated from college with a degree in business management. For all the money thrown his way, including the Range Rover parked outside, he wasn't as smart as Rosie. The child who went to an estate school in clothes that were often too tight for her. She was only able to take GCE's but managed to average A's – B+ in all curriculum subjects. Michael scraped his degree and spent most of his time with girls or up to no good.

Mildred had syphoned money for him all her married life as well as herself. Neither had ever gone without a thing. Walter had worked to keep them for over twenty-five years. He'd no real idea of the struggles Rosie had faced. He hadn't blamed her one bit for leaving home as soon as she'd scraped together a rental deposit. He'd had no control over joint money but at least he'd made sure she was fed and watered under his roof. Rightly or wrongly, he had thought it was best to wait until she was twenty-five before passing on his inheritance to her. She never told him how bad things really were for her, he didn't know.

She never held it against him or asked for anything. She was a good girl and shared not only his hair colour, even if his was salt and pepper now and very faded! But also. his temperament, she was laid back and friendly.

Rosie and Anna walked to the Village Hall. The workmen were working seven days a week on the best rates to get the jobs done. Rosie had given them a four to five week deadline; ensuring she got the best deals for Dorothea's money. The roof, wiring, plumbing, updated heating, kitchen fitments were all well under way. Jane was picking her colour schemes and choosing her furniture from the comfort of her London flat.

Rosie was mindful to keep in mind that one day she might have a family. The ground floor would have a kitchen, bathroom, lounge, one double and two single bedrooms. All of it neutral colours. For now, she was going to use a corner of the lounge as an office. Once she was settled in, her priority was going to be sorting through Dorothea's papers. She was going to 'investigate' the family as such. Including her Nana.

Two men sat in the corner of the Flag public house. Plotting and planning. Their wives had gone off to that jumble sale this afternoon.

"I drove past there this afternoon. We haven't got a chance of getting inside the Garden Centre now. I knew we should have struck right away. What if the pearls *are* there?" Jack asked.

"Stop whinging, why don't you. There's always the B & B. Granted, we still can't get near the place for now. Chances are what we're looking for is more likely to be *there* anyway. I told you before, leave all this to me. We will get what's ours and I don't care who cops it on the way. Our women may have failed, but we won't." Steven replied. Jack and Steven supped their pints.

~

Michael Smith and his mother, Mildred Wodehouse, left London at one o'clock. They intended to reach Bromington-on-sea at tea-time. Mildred had booked two rooms at the Lobster Pot public house. They were due to drive home Monday morning. For now, Michael was stopping with her at the bungalow. After all, it was in his best financial interests to help in any way he could.

Meeting the villagers

There was something which always hits you first inside village halls. An echo. The loudness of shoes on floorboards. A traditional kitchen with a tea urn boiled out the back somewhere and a couple of toilets were always to hand. Bromington Village Hall turned out to be something of a community centre. Children came here a couple of nights a week when the space was used for table tennis and badminton; on a Monday and a Friday, it was a youth club selling fizzy drinks and crisps. Bridge night was on a Thursday. The W.I claimed the hall on Tuesday evenings. Wednesdays was a free for all. Sometimes council meetings were held and once-in-a-while a medium made an appearance. Saturday evenings were kept free for occasional social gatherings. But, not on jumble afternoons. Apparently, they hosted a very good local band. They weren't licensed to sell alcohol, but you could bring your own. Sundays, the hall was shut. The only gathering on that day, for those so inclined, was a Sunday morning service at the church on top of the hill. Sybil was feeding the newcomers all the info.

"I feel we know the place so well already! Thank you, Sybil."

"You're very welcome, Rosie; let me introduce you to a few of the ladies and gents."

Rosie thanked her and Anna trailed behind, her eyes feasting everywhere at once, looking for the bargains of the day. With a quick glance, Rosie noted mostly trestle tables full of clothes which were scrabbled about by the early birds. One table had an assortment of knitted baby clothes and booties arranged in neat sets. Several home-made cakes and pastries adorned the centre table-top, together with home-made everything, in various sized jars. Jewellery, pottery, gifts, shoes, boots and a rail at the back housing several furs. Which rang a bell. Perhaps the fox fur stoles *were* full of fleas. Maybe Dorothea had bequeathed everything from a local jumble sale and no doubt the pearls were a worthless imitation. Rosie smiled at the thought!

Two women nudged each other.

"Look, it's her."

"Yes, and there's the other one, over there."

"Stay close to them, listen to what they say."

"Good idea. That busybody Sybil will no doubt introduce them to everyone."

"Let's not despair. We spent too much time sucking up to the old biddy."

"Shame we weren't there the day she died. It would have made things so much easier!"

"I've told you before, I looked for the pearls high and low when you distracted her. I couldn't find them."

"Well, we could have looked a bit harder if she was dead, couldn't we?"

"Don't have a go at me. Your husband shouldn't have put them down in the first place, should he!"

"Sandra, you know the customs men were scouring the harbour. Steven thought by putting them on the jumble jewellery table for a few minutes nobody would have a chance to look at them! Anyway, Duncan suggested he did it."

"Well he thought wrong, Jennifer. The old biddy selling them had no idea what they were, £20 she charged, and I had no chance of retrieving them. That Sybil was with her, they went straight inside her shopping trolley. With some of them horrible furs and other rubbish."

"We know all this, she drove Dorothea home and we were masquerading as cleaners for weeks after, trying to find them. I reckon she must have a safe somewhere."

"If it wasn't for the watchmen hired to watch the place, we could have broken in."

"And if they hadn't found the family, the stuff would have gone to charity and we might have located them."

"All ifs and buts. I have an idea though, follow me!"

"What are you going to do, Sandra?" Jennifer watched her friend walk away, over to the new women.

"Excuse me, I couldn't help but overhear. Did you say you were a relative of dear Mrs Wodehouse? My name is Helen."

"Miss Wodehouse, yes," Rosie smiled. "Did you know her?"

"Oh, very well. What a shame, terrible it was. Here one minute, gone the next. We used to be her house-keepers you see," Helen replied. Which wasn't her name at all.

"Really? I don't recall seeing you before," Sybil smiled, with a smile not reaching her eyes.

"It was only for a few weeks, and then sadly she passed away. We aren't here all the time. We sail a lot you see, with our husbands. My name's Janice," said the other lady. Which was another lie.

"Yes, we all bumped into each other one day at the harbour and Mrs, er, Miss Wodehouse explained how she could do with a bit of help once a week. Big house like that needs a lot of looking after." 'Helen' explained.

"Which got us to thinking. We intend to be around for a few weeks, so if you are looking for any casual help, cash in hand like, cleaning up – you will find us moored up down the end there, seeing as we already know the place and everything." 'Janice' offered.

"I'll keep it in mind, thank you. We might need a bit of help when all the work's finished." Rosie smiled.

"I think it will take you weeks going through Dorothea's personal belongings!" Anna laughed. She had probably said the wrong thing in the present company.

"Well, nice to meet you both. I'll be in touch. Rosie has left me to do all the hiring and firing for the moment." Sybil took a surprised Rosie by the arm and went to introduce her to Judith. Her friend who runs the jewellery stall.

"That's news to me," Rosie whispered to Sybil.

"Sorry, my dear, but there's something about those two that doesn't sit right. Dorothea didn't tell me about casual cleaners. Mind you, she was a little vacant over the last few weeks. Even so, I can't see her approaching them, besides, she only came to the village when I drove her here."

Jennifer and Sandra left the building, or in this case the Village Hall. Maybe their husbands might be able to worm their way in somehow. They headed off to the Flag to meet Jack and

Steven armed with nothing more than pots of marmalade. The two couples carried on trying to hatch a plan.

"Let's see now. I will put a card in that newsagents. Painters and decorators. Stands to reason they'll be looking for some. I overheard a bit of small talk. Money's no object with doing up the big house."

"Good idea, Jack. A less direct approach than Sandra's. If there is a wall safe hidden, we'll have valid excuses for taking paintings down."

"Got it in one, Steven. And if we don't find them there then we need to break into that Garden Centre."

A good hour later the ladies left the Village Hall.

"We will have to come here again, Rosie. Miranda has some lovely rolls of fabric. I think Mum will love these reds and purples. I can see her making her own floor length curtains and bed quilt. That will save some money from your 'Great Aunt Dorothea's' funds. I got these for a great price!" Anna had it all piled up in an old coach pram. Well, for £5, the buggy would come in handy going backwards and forwards on jumble days.

"I love the house plants. I got some for all of us, be careful pushing that thing. It's not as if you've had any practise!" Rosie thought it was a great idea though. The basket underneath was the perfect place for the greenery. With several bags hanging from the handle the two friends set off back to their B & B.

Sybil remained in her van. She was watching the folk sitting in the Flag watching the two friends walk away from the village. Something didn't sit right with them and she decided to stay where she was, holding her newspaper up to her face. Of all the boats in the harbour, Sybil was particularly interested to know which one they were heading back to. She didn't have long to wait. Somewhere in the boot, Derek had a good pair of binoculars. He used them for bird watching along the riverbanks. Jolly good they were too. Sybil zoomed in and it was almost as if she were standing right behind the foursome. At least she knew which boat they boarded. The fourth one along.

Next up she was taking a stroll over to the newsagents, she had seen one of the men put a card in the bottom corner of the shop window. What was all that about she wondered? A little while later, Sybil drove off, taking the longer road past the harbour. She went home to tell Derek all about her suspicions. The two ladies, Helen and Janice, their husbands. The painting and decorating card and a boat moored up called 'Lazy Daze'.

"I quite agree, Sybil. Very unlike Dorothea to hire help in the street."

"She did get a bit confused over the last few months though. Take the linens. They'd been passed down through the generations and I'm sure she never meant for them to go to this Mildred Wodehouse, who by all accounts, was no better in her eyes than Walter's mother. Although, he seems such a lovely chap. We never did get to the bottom of that!"

"I think, as you say, Sybil, she muddled them up with the old stuff from the jumble, you know with the second-hand pearls and musty old furs! I'm glad you posted them and got them out of Riverside Cottage. Oh, and that reminds me, I've told everyone else. Walter doesn't want to see that wife of his anymore. Had enough of her by all accounts and will be starting divorce proceedings. Anyway, this is a picture of her. If she ever comes by, we are to say he sleeps in the back of the café on a pullout camp bed and Riverside Cottage is our home."

Sybil couldn't help laughing. "She really must be a bit of an old dragon then. I know Dorothea hired a team some while back, investigators of some sort. She was very sure only Walter and his daughter would ever truly benefit from her estate."

"Sybil, why don't you just share out the antique linens with you and that nice lady, Jane? I'm sure neither Rosie nor Walter will have any objections. At least you will both appreciate them. Anyway, don't you worry about these boat people. I'll have a word with, Duncan, the harbour master. See if we can't find out a little more."

Neither Derek nor Sybil had any idea the pearls Dorothea paid £20 for, which had been sitting on a chair for months on end, were worth a small fortune. They thought, along with the other worthless toot, they had gone to this Mildred Wodehouse, in London somewhere. Meanwhile, at the B & B, the friends were chatting.

"What do you think of the locals then, Anna?"

"Well, let me see if I can remember them all. Judith runs the jewellery stall. Miranda sells the beautiful materials. Roger brings along his wonderful indoor and outdoor plants. Mrs. Iris Jackson runs the bakers and sells some of her cakes, bread and pastries at the jumble on Saturday mornings, only her daughter Liz, who was very funny by the way, sets up her stall. Also, when there's a local fete at the school."

Rosie added, "Barney runs the newsagents and sends all the stuff reaching its sell-by date to the jumble, where his son, Richard, sellotapes raffle ticket numbers on the items, five tickets for a £1. Any number ending in zero or five is a winner. I did manage to win us a box of chocolates, out of date in two weeks- time." Rosie was as happy with all their booty as Anna. "I didn't like those women in the hall, the ones from the harbour."

"Neither did I, Rosie Boo-boo. We better get all this stuff back and then pop over to the Garden Centre before we get locked out!"

"Don't you mean Fort Knox! It is a good idea though, plus the security lights and alarm system for the B & B. You can never be too careful!" As they were about to cross the road to their new home, something caught their attention. A flash of light in the top window, reflecting the sun, as if someone was holding a mirror towards the road.

At six o'clock that evening a Range Rover slowed down to a crawl and the two occupants got a good look at the building surrounded with scaffolding. It didn't look like anyone was home. Apart from one man and a dog disappearing around the side of the building.

"Looks like a security guard, Michael."

"Yes, Mother. And the garden place was gated. I don't think we're going to see much this weekend."

"Don't be so sure of that. Let's get to this Lobster Pot place. If we don't let on who we are we, we might catch some useful gossip."

"Something's going on. The fact neither Rosie nor your husband have been available since they left…"

"Yes, and there wasn't even a note with my inheritance…"

"Do you think they planned this Mother? Maybe they've always known this aunt was leaving them something and neither you nor I was going to get any of it. Well, apart from the pearl necklace. Have you had it valued?"

"Not yet. I did bring it with me though. The stoles might have been worth something, but not at the expense of riddling me with fleas. The binmen have taken them, and the grotty chair back covers and other rubbish. Don't worry, I will sort this."

A blunt reception

After a miserable and unproductive evening, Mildred had retired to her room. Michael had insisted taking the large front room with the sea view; so, he could keep an eye on things. Who would have thought two pokey rooms would cost so much and the price of two fish meals was atrocious.

Now Mildred was footing the bill for everything, she realised how expensive her son could be. He never put his hand in his pocket, for anything. To top it all, the small window in her room overlooked a noisy extractor fan and bins. The shared bathroom was up the hall. The threadbare hall carpet was no match for the luxurious Wilton in the main hallway and pub area.

Mildred's slippers stuck to the carpet as she carried her thin, small towel and toiletry bag along the dark hallway. She shared her top room with two other occupants behind the brown doors with flaked paint.

The bathroom was cold and musty, but at least she'd got there first. She'd noticed another pub along the road. The Flag. As she hadn't paid for the rooms yet, she was going to walk along there and see if they had anything more suitable. One night at the Lobster Pot was one night too many. The sink tap dripped and was tight. When she brushed her teeth hardly any water came out of the tap. The shower was freezing cold for a good ten minutes then switched to scalding hot. There didn't seem to be anything in-between.

Breakfast was passable, but Mildred complained about anything and everything served to her. Stale tea, bitter coffee, cold toast, hard eggs, fatty bacon, soggy cereal, watery juice.

"How was your room, Michael?"

"Wonderful, Mother; the bed was comfortable, the en-suite spacious and the view is quite spectacular."

"You can stay here if you want to, but I'm going to book myself in along the road tonight. I'm not paying to stay here another night."

A frown passed over Michael's face. Maybe it would be worth him paying for the second night here out of his own pocket. Personally, he'd enjoyed his breakfast as well. Besides, it might be a good idea for him to distance himself this evening. He wanted to see if there was any local talent in Bromington-on-sea, a weekend fling. His mother was cramping his style.

"Why don't you let me ask for you? Maybe you can take a bit of time looking around the village this morning. See what you can find out?"

"I don't want any old room. If they have one, I want a sea view and a private bathroom. It doesn't matter what they have for you, after all, I'm paying."

Michael half-smiled and caught the eye of the waitress as she walked past. He didn't look away and neither did she. No, he didn't have any intention of going anywhere. As soon as he went back to his room, he rang the Flag. "Do you have a nice en-suite room available this evening with a sea view. Single or double, it doesn't matter. You do? That's wonderful. Mrs Wodehouse, one night."

Michael walked upstairs and knocked on his mother's door. It was dark upstairs, not like the middle floor.

"You're all booked in Mother. If you settle the bill for last night's rooms, I will pay for my own tonight. I've got you the Flag's best room, they only had one, so I'm happy to stay here!"

"Oh, but I didn't really mean for us to be in separate places, Michael," Mildred complained.

"Don't worry about it, you pack your things up and I'll be happy to explain to the manager. I will carry your case for you, see you at eleven at reception." Michael spun on his heel and headed downstairs to square things with the waitress.

"Well, I'm very sorry your mum's room wasn't up to scratch. To be honest they only let upstairs out when the rest is fully booked. We won't charge her for it," Betsie smiled.

Michael was wondering how he could wangle his room for two nights at the expense of his mother if she didn't know that snippet of information.

"Can you write me a bill with just the total for my room for two nights. I'll pay it in cash. No need to be too specific, just give me the receipt please. What time do you finish work? I was wondering if you might like to show me around?"

Betsie smiled. "After lunch, then I'm free for the rest of the day. Back on duty tomorrow lunch-time."

"That's sorted then. I'll settle mother in down the road at eleven and I'll meet you where? What time?"

"I can meet you down by the harbour, say two o'clock? I need to go home first and get ready."

"It's a date," Michael grinned. *Or a one night stand* he thought. Whichever way you looked at it. He headed off for a shower and a shave. His mother wanted to visit the Garden Centre straight after her check in at the Flag. He'd be sure she went to the cashpoint too, to pay him back for the bill he'd paid. Michael had no real interest in finding Walter, or Rosie. He couldn't care less if he never clapped eyes on either one again. The only reason he was here was the lure of money, nothing else. In fact, once he got any sort of pay-off he rather fancied a stint in Australia himself. His mother would be quite capable of looking after herself. A qualified man, the right age group, he always toyed with emigrating. Which wasn't an option for someone of Mildred's age anyway. His mother had lied to Walter all these years, she knew his real father's surname.

An unusual surname at that, Fernsby. Michael had done a bit of research during his college years, and he was pretty sure he'd traced his father. Blond. Married. Three children. Own business. A house with a pool. When Michael drained his mother and her husband dry, someone he never thought of as his father, he'd move onto pastures new. He would start all over again. After all, his real father owed him.

Walter drove his jaguar just before lunch, with his gardening tools in the boot. Anna and Rosie followed behind. No sooner had they turned off via a shortcut they now knew, Mildred Wodehouse and Michael Smith drove into the Garden Centre a few minutes later, they'd been travelling on the main road. Mildred Wodehouse had no intention of leaving today without some sort of explanation and at the very least a handsome pay-off. It was obvious, even to her, Walter had no intention of coming home. Maybe she could talk him into handing over the bungalow to her, which she would then promptly sell.

Mildred slammed the car door, her adrenaline pumping through her veins and marched off towards the café. She had no interest in browsing fields of boring plants, looking for her husband. Riverside Cottage caught her beady eye straight away. Was that the accommodation?

Derek was pottering about watering tubs when he spotted them. Him and his good wife, Sybil, hatched a plan just the evening before and now he knew his wife would need a few minutes to 'prepare'.

"Good morning, Madam, can I help you?" he called loudly. Sybil looked out of the café window and sprang into action in the stock room.

"I'm looking for a Mr. Walter Wodehouse," Mildred sharply replied.

"Walter, you say. Can't say that rings any bells. Does he work here?"

"Work here?" Mildred scoffed. "He owns the place. His Aunt Dorothea left it to him in her will. Where is he?"

"Oh, that Walter! I do beg your pardon. I only met him once briefly. He didn't stay long you see."

"What do you mean, didn't stay long? Does he live here or doesn't he?"

"And who are you, exactly?"

"Who do you think I am! I'm his wife of course."

"Oh, you must be Mildred. He asked my wife to post a parcel down to you. We do hope it arrived safely."

"Yes, it did. And the contents went straight in the bin."

"Oh, that looked like a nice necklace Dorothea had left you."

"Apart from that, the rest went in the bin. Now, where is he? Is that his house?" Mildred pointed to Riverside Cottage.

"That? Oh no. That's our house that is, it belongs to me and my wife. It was my parents before that."

"Well, where does Walter live then?"

"He doesn't live here, we do. There is sleeping accommodation on site for the owner to use, would you like to see it?"

"Yes. And then I want a word or two with that husband of mine!" Mildred bellowed.

"Sybil dear, could you show this lady Walter's, accommodation, this is his wife. But I don't know if there's quite room enough for two." Walter gave a wink to Sybil in the café.

"Very pleased to meet you, I'm sure. Come this way." Sybil walked past the private bathroom and into the storeroom. There amongst tins and jars, toilet rolls and hanging baskets was a fold down bed. It hadn't been slept in. A curtain rail with a few empty hangers faced Mildred in this 10 x 12-foot room.

"Walter declined the offer to stay. I do believe he has gone away for a few weeks while his daughter has her new Bed and Breakfast refurbished. So, for now, Derek and I shall continue managing the Garden Centre as Dorothea instructed," Sybil explained.

"That's right. The old house needs major repair work doing. We don't know anything more, sorry." Derek shrugged. "I think you've had a bit of a wasted journey, would you like a cup of tea?"

"No thank you. We've had quite enough at the village pub," Michael answered.

"Are you Walter's son?" Sybil asked, innocently.

"No," Michael replied. "My father lives in Australia."

"Oh, I see. Silly of me to think it really. You aren't a red-head like his lovely daughter." Sybil was on full form.

"Well, enjoy your stay in the village, are you here long?" Derek asked.

"One more night. Where did you say he had gone?" Mildred barked.

"Wales, I think he said," Sybil replied. "Excuse me, I have customers."

"His daughter too?" Mildred asked. Derek could not figure out how someone as mild-mannered as Walter had put up with this awful woman for so long.

"Yes, they've gone together. Walter said they'd never had a proper holiday. Well, I must get back to work. Nice meeting you both." Walter gestured for them to leave. As soon as they pulled away, he rang Walter.

"Your wife was just here. She's in Bromington until tomorrow. We told her you and Rosie were in Wales and showed her the stock room, saying you had declined it, just as we planned. She thinks Riverside Cottage belongs to us. She was with the blond-haired man, who, I take it is your son. Only according to him, you aren't his dad, his dad lives in Australia. Not only that, your wife refers to Rosie as *your* daughter. For what it's worth, Walter, I think you have done the right thing.

Walter thanked him. "Mother's arrived. And Michael, they've just left the Garden Centre. We must have narrowly missed them."

"Don't worry, Dad. I'll get security to guard the front door and block the way around to the parking rea. We don't want them seeing our cars." Rosie rushed off to explain to Nigel.

Anna knew why her friend was doing this. Psychologically, Walter was in a good place. He needed to stay there, stay strong. True to form, within ten minutes, a car tried to pull up on the drive. Nigel stopped it in his tracks. "No admittance here; this is private property."

"I'm looking for my sister, Rosie Wodehouse," Michael explained.

"Well, you won't find her here. Now, turn around and don't come back. There is some underpinning going on here and the building is dangerous. As far as I know the new owner won't be back for several months."

Nigel told even bigger porkies than the rest of them. The house would be ready for occupation within the month.

"Well." Mildred huffed. "I can't see absolutely any point whatsoever staying in this awful place a moment longer. We may as well go home."

"Don't be hasty, Mother. Besides, I've paid for my room at the Lobster Pot, and you had to pay for your room in advance at the Flag. Both are non-refundable. You get yourself a bit of sea air and leave me to find out what I can while I'm here." Michael wasn't going anywhere, at least not until tomorrow. He was looking forward to a room-service breakfast after an evening out with today's waitress. He was hoping tomorrow's waitress was just as attractive and he wouldn't be disturbed.

The missing person

Mildred Wodehouse woke up with one of her heads. She'd not had one like this since... she couldn't remember when. A hangover is what she had, to be precise. Her mouth was as dry as a bone. The room was spinning, and no sooner had she turned her head, her whole body felt nauseous. The digital clock on the dresser showed her it was 8:39. However she had got back to her room was a mystery. She had no recollection of anything after nine o'clock last night. As soon as that noisy band came on at full blast.

She remembered Michael dropping her back to the hotel before he went off to find information about Dorothea Wodehouse.

She remembered someone shouting, a woman. Who was that? Mildred tried to rack her brains. It all started when she ate, around four in the afternoon. A glass of wine had seemed like a good idea at the time. And then another. By tea-time she was quite merry. Around seven o'clock she felt hungry and ate some sort of dessert. Then she drank some more. A little wobbly on her feet, but not out of control.

Next thing she was outside with a whole bottle of wine and talking to heaven knows who. Everything else was just a blur. She did remember someone shouting again. A snippet of her complaining about her husband, she told a woman all she got was some pearls. And then Mildred got very confused.

She remembered feeling chilly and now it was morning. Here she was in the room at the Flag. Her clothes were thrown on the floor and if she wasn't mistaken, she'd been sick on the carpet.

Michael woke up refreshed, rejuvenated. The waitress had shown him plenty of local attractions and he'd had a productive evening. Unfortunately, room service was delivered by a man this morning. Still, not to worry. The town beckoned and he'd been more than satisfied with his seaside visit. All in all, it had been an eventful evening.

Mildred fell back to sleep, awoken at ten a.m. by the sound of someone shouting. She reached for the decanter of water by her bed and drunk greedily. She'd missed breakfast but had no desire to eat anything anyway.

With a weak stomach she gingerly stepped out of bed, she had to clean the mess up, perhaps a tepid shower would make her feel better. She was meeting Michael at eleven and was not looking forward to the journey home. Not in this state.

The pub was a mess. Last orders had been just before one o'clock the night before. At this time a string of taxis arrived to take home the late-night revellers. Thank goodness the 70's band were only booked once a year. Everyone came from miles around. With their Tina Turner wigs and Elton John glasses it was a popular, but very noisy event. *Glamrockers* certainly knew how to get the crowd going. A lot of the locals turned up, those in walking distance anyway, everyone else was from far and wide.

~

Walter had been toying with the idea of telling Rosie about the pearls. He'd no idea of their worth until he went to a jewellers in a large nearby town. When he explained they'd been bequeathed by his aunt and who he was, it seemed good enough for the jeweller. Any relative of Dorothea Wodehouse was welcome in his shop, he'd said. The pearls had papers in the box and no doubt the lady of great wealth had accumulated them on her travels. Ivan, the jeweller, quite understood why a man didn't want them. The money was much more agreeable. The jeweller couldn't believe his luck. Life had just gotten so much easier. Walter had no idea of what he was selling and there was a buyer waiting. Cash would be transferred and the jeweller could retire. Even the buyer had a buyer. In fact, they'd already claimed the insurance for their unique missing pearls. So, the dealing was very, hush-hush. The only reason Walter got an eighth of the real value was because the jeweller wrongly presumed he already knew they were very valuable.

Walter had then gone to another jewellers and purchased the cheap pearls. He shouldn't have felt guilty. His wife would have sold the originals immediately, and he wouldn't have seen a penny of the money, of that he was sure. No, what stumped him was, Dorothea obviously had no feeling for Mildred. So, why on earth would she give her something so valuable?

A little while ago he had a quarter of a million pounds. Most of that he had given to his daughter. Now he had twice as much as he did a few weeks ago. It didn't make sense. Was he doing the right thing keeping the cash? Should he give Mildred a part of it? His mind was all in a quandary. Most people worried about a lack of money, not too much of it! Perhaps Sybil could put him wise. Maybe he should have a quiet chat with her first?

Off he went to the café. Hopefully Mildred wouldn't come back, but his jaguar was in the workshop out of sight for the day and Rosie and Anna had set off for a day's sightseeing. While Walter and Sybil sat chatting in the café, Michael's Range Rover shot past at full speed heading back to London.

"I hope you don't mind, Sybil, but I wanted to ask you about the stuff Dorothea bequeathed to Mildred."

"Oh, I'm so sorry, Walter. I know I shouldn't have, but Dorothea did get all in a muddle the weeks before she passed. I think the linens were not the ones we got at the jumble. So, I swapped them over before you posted the parcel."

"Jumble?"

"Well, yes. I didn't like to say it, but Dorothea had been doing a bit of digging around, you know; she hired some investigators, and well, she wanted to know all about you. After your mother died, she changed. She didn't like her and never wanted her to be a part of any will. Don't ask me why, I don't know. Truly.

So, whatever she found out about your Mildred, she didn't take a liking to her at all, or Michael. But not you. She knew you had a gardening business and all your customers spoke highly of you. She found out about Rosie living alone and struggling. The more she found out about your daughter, the more she liked her resilience, stamina and determination. She is a lot like Dorothea in her ways.

She had a vision. For you, for Rosie, but not your wife and certainly not your son. So, one day she asked me to take her to the jumble. She picked up the pearls, fox furs and some old linens and we left. She wanted to leave Mildred worthless junk. To make a statement."

"So, she didn't know anything about the pearls?"

"Didn't give them a second glance. We took it all back to hers until she asked me a few days later to put them to one side, here at the cottage. She said if they were claimed I was to give them to Mildred."

"So, it was never Dorothea's intention to give Mildred anything of any value?"

"Oh no, just the opposite. She was of the impression you'd given her and Michael enough over the years. And forgive me for saying, but I don't think your wife was very true to you."

"Do you remember who sold her the pearls?"

"Oh, that's easy enough. She brought them from Judith. She's always run the jewellery stall. But, to be honest, she didn't recall having them for sale, but was happy to take £20 for them. They didn't have a price see. Usually everything does."

"And they were definitely the ones you left on the chair with the furs? I don't mind at all if you swapped the linens. Knowing my wife, she would have thrown all of it straight in the bin."

"Saved me a job then, they weren't even good enough for me to donate to the jumble to be honest. Why do you ask, Walter?"

"No reason, really. I would hate to think my wife was sent anything of any value just for her to throw them in a bin. I'd rather wear them myself!"

Sybil threw her head back and laughed so much her belly ached. Wiping tears from her eyes, she simply said, "that's funny! I've met your wife and all I can say is the investigators were right."

"How long have you and Derek worked here, Sybil?"

"All our working lives and very happy we are. You will have to come to us one day for tea. We have a cottage very similar to the one you have here. It was tied, came with the job, but nearer to the nature reserve. Derek loves it there. Just like you, we were bequeathed. We got a lump sum and the cottage a few years before Dorothea passed away. I'm glad about that, because she was of sound mind then, she meant us to have them."

"Wasn't she of sound mind at the end?"

"Not for a few months. Take those cleaners down the harbour; I still don't believe she asked them to go to her house every week cleaning. She had a daily. My sister. Well, three days a week she went. Now they have the brass neck to ask your Rosie if they can come back to clean again. Their husbands have put up a card advertising themselves as painters. They're up to no good! Mark my words. I watched them yesterday, on a boat called Lazy Daze they are."

"Thank you, Sybil. I'll speak with Rosie. Can I ask, did Dorothea leave you comfortable?"

"Oh yes, she did. We only work here because we like it so much. We don't need the money, Walter. Dorothea also had her marbles when she changed her will, benefitting you and Rosie." Sybil clutched his arm, reassuringly.

Walter drove off to the B & B. He loved working in the garden there. Well, maybe he'd wait a couple of weeks before talking with Rosie about the pearls. First off, he'd make sure Rosie didn't take on the cleaners or the painters. In fact, as soon as the rewiring and plastering was dry, he would do it all himself. Or better still, perhaps they would all chip in. Knowing the three ladies as he did, he was sure there would be nothing they'd like better. If Sybil's sister still wanted to clean at the B & B, Rosie could employ her.

It was very quiet today, but no sooner had he thought that, Walter heard loud sirens.

Come Tuesday morning the news was all over Bromington-on-sea. A woman's body had been found washed up with the tide yesterday. According to unofficial reports, it would seem she had taken a fall off the cliff edge, not thirty yards away from the church. The area had a fence, and everybody knew not to go past it.

The police had the area cordoned off around the top of the cliff, although several tourists would have walked as far as the fencing most days. It was a great place to snap photographs and lots of people had been to the village over the weekend. There had been a formal identification, but details weren't being released yet. Not until after a post-mortem. For now, the circumstances were unclear.

Everybody in Bromington was in shock. All of them waiting for news. A few people were around for the band at the Flag, Sunday evening, most of them drunk, a few locals, and not so local. It could have been anyone a little worse for wear who'd wandered off.

Mildred and Michael caught the end of the story on the morning news back at the London bungalow. Mildred wasn't in the least bit concerned; her daughter was in Wales. Even if she hadn't been, she wasn't in the slightest bit worried. The first thought that went through her head was to wonder who would get the B & B if something happened to Rosalyn.

~

"Mum don't worry. We're both fine. Rosie is sitting here with me right now." Anna assured her concerned mother.

"I'm right here, Jane, it seems like a tragic accident; maybe someone got too close to the edge," Rosie called out.

"Promise me you two will stay away from that area. We need to make sure little Bear doesn't wander near cliff edges. How dreadful." Jane was shocked. Also, a little worried. It could have been suicide, or worse than that, a murder.

"We promise. I don't think it's going to be anyone we know. We have spoken with Sybil this morning and everyone who runs the jumble is fine." Anna was making all the right noises to calm her mum down. "Anyway, Mum, I think it's going to be alright for us to pop back in a couple of days and finish packing. The floors have been sanded, cleaned and buffed. The new kitchens are in, so are the bathrooms."

"Yes, and we've been talking to Dad, Jane. He thinks we can get the new furniture delivered. If you can put up with a little chaos, how about we book a removal van for this weekend and we all do our own finishing touches. Paints, curtains, all of that. Besides, I'm missing my pets!" Rosie chirped.

"The B & B half will have a refurbishment afterwards. Rosie decided in the end to give the house priority. The teams have made excellent progress!" Anna said with great enthusiasm.

Neither of them mentioned the fact Mildred had been down with Michael, probably looking to cause a scene. Or the fact things seemed to go bump in the broad daylight. A tragedy was a little unnerving to say the least. Everyone felt it would be nice to finally regroup.

"Dad, can we get a final spurt on, do you think? Would it be possible to get a few more hands in? We've sort of promised Jane we'd be down to see her in a couple of days and can book the removal for this weekend. Now I need to urgently get some beds and sofas."

"Leave it with me, girls. If Derek and Sybil can't help out with people they know, I'll eat my hat!"

"You don't have a hat!" Rosie gave him a big cuddle and started ringing around.

An accidental death

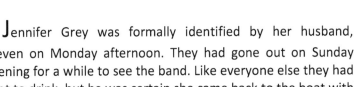

Jennifer Grey was formally identified by her husband, Steven on Monday afternoon. They had gone out on Sunday evening for a while to see the band. Like everyone else they had a lot to drink, but he was certain she came back to the boat with him and they went to bed around midnight. No, they hadn't been up on the hill, he said. If he was perfectly honest, he didn't remember much after ten-thirty. When told the function was on until one o'clock, he was no longer certain what time they came home. He was so drunk he didn't even remember if his wife was there on the boat or not, or if she was with him at the pub.

His friends, Jack and Sandra Hughes told the police in their statement they came home earlier that evening and went to bed. The harbour was so noisy, there was even fireworks, so they had no clue what time Jennifer and Steven got back, or if they came back together. They went out at ten o'clock Monday morning, which they always did and then headed off for a day out together. When they got back, there was a lot of police activity and Steven had mistakenly thought Jennifer had been out with them all day.

It wasn't until then he told the police his wife might be missing. Steven was known to lose his temper when the drink took hold and he was racking his brains trying to piece Sunday night together. With the waves of crushing grief rushing over him he couldn't think straight.

Sandra made one pot of tea after another, clearly shaken by what was going on. The harbour was unusually quiet. The people on the boat were villagers, more or less; even though they'd only been around for a few months, on and off. When Sybil saw the picture in the local paper on Wednesday, she knew she had been right to mistrust them. Janice, she'd said her name was, and the other one called herself Helen. Why lie? Rosie and Anna had gone back to London for a few days. Maybe the young woman could begin to piece it all together when she came back. Put her enquiring mind to the test.

The police confirmed there was a high level of alcohol in Jennifer Grey's body and they weren't treating the death as suspicious at this stage. It seemed it was a tragic accident. No other footprints were found behind the cordoned off area and the woman wasn't dead before she fell. Her lungs were full of water. Apart from a bashing to the side of her head caused by rocks on the way down there were no other marks. She hadn't been strangled, stabbed or assaulted. As the area was dark at night there were no witnesses in that end of the village. Police were calling for anyone who remembered seeing Jennifer on that Sunday night.

The only person who thought it all looked very suspicious, was Sybil. But still, she had work to do, as did Derek. Her sister, Betty, was filling in at the Garden Centre café this week. They had to pull some strings locally to get beds and sofas delivered, they were off to pick up paint in the colours chosen by the ladies. For now, it was taking their minds off goings-on in the village. It used to be very quiet around here, now the place was buzzing with anticipation. June was earmarked for the B & B to be back in business.

After being home for two or three days, Mildred realised she no longer had her pearls. She'd taken them to Bromington with her, even though she hadn't worn them. She had double checked everything when she left the Lobster Pot. Not so much when checking out of the Flag. Michael was suddenly impatient to get back home, and she put her bag together in a hurry. The weekend had been a total waste of time and had infuriated her to the extreme. Two days it had taken her to recover from the terrible hangover. No wonder there were rooms available at the Flag. Anyone with any sense wouldn't have stayed there on such a busy night.

Mildred's condition hadn't improved on Monday. She hadn't felt better as the day went on, she had little appetite until Wednesday. If anything, she felt like she had been drugged outside the Flag pub on Sunday evening.

Of course, it wasn't any help to find no CCTV on the harbour side of Bromington-on-sea. The Lobster Pot public house thought it was a waste of money. Neither the bakers nor the newsagents could see any benefit to it and the Flag manager thought it would just cause unnecessary aggravation among the customers if there was ever a ruckus.

Mildred decided to change tack. On Saturday afternoon she planned on getting her male friend, Arthur, to drive her over to the flats where Rosie and Anna lived. There might be a chance that arty-farty woman upstairs might know the whereabouts of Rosie and Walter. Or she may be gullible enough to hand over their new phone numbers, because they certainly were not using their old ones anymore. The numbers were no longer in service.

Arthur had been with Mildred for many years. There had never been an Audrey. While Walter had spent his life working for his family even though he brought up another man's son, his wife had been getting her jollies elsewhere.

In fact, she was no different to Walter's mother, who unbeknown to Walter, had indirectly caused the accident that killed his father. His father's car had come off the road because he was speeding along to catch his wife in the act with her lover. One his sister, Dorothea, had warned him about. She had spotted her with different men on several occasions, but they hadn't noticed her. On that fateful day, Dorothea had seen Sylvia Wodehouse, Walter's mother, go off with a man to a hotel.

Dorothea never told anyone the truth. She felt guilty her whole life, if not for her, then her dear brother, William, would not have died. He had not wanted to believe her, this time she insisted he went and saw it for himself. Neither her parents, nor Sylvia Wodehouse were aware of her knowledge.

To make things worse, straight after her brother's death, Sylvia Wodehouse ended her trivial affair. At the end of the day it had meant that little to her. She did not question why her sister-in-law had no more to do with her, but Sylvia must have had a good idea.

In a roundabout way, Dorothea Wodehouse always wanted to make it up to Walter. The boy who grew up fatherless, because of her. But, there was no way on God's Earth Sylvia Wodehouse would benefit from Dorothea, she'd had more than enough money from her parents. And, in turn, there was no way Mildred, the disgrace of a mother to her own daughter and the cheating wife of Walter, would ever get a penny either.

Dorothea Wodehouse took all her secrets to her lonely grave. She only shared them in her diary. The one she could not locate in the months before her death. Her mind was betraying her.

~

Come Saturday morning, everything was loaded from Jane's flat. Her friends and neighbours were all more than willing to lend a hand. She had donated items to charity over the last couple of weeks, given away odds and ends she really didn't need anymore, and packed with great care all her personal possessions. Everything which was going with her was now in the back of the removal van.

Jane was driving to Bromington in the van with Bumble in a cage on the floor and Rosie strapped in with little Bear. It was going to be a slow journey with several stops!

Anna's boot was filled with hers and Rosie's clothes and the two friends were having a good tidy up. Bear and Bumble were there with them. Bear was running around both flats, up and down the stairs and making lots of mischief! Bumble was very sulky, already in the cage, waiting to go.

At least they'd saved two parking spaces this morning. With the help of two of the neighbours and Anna taking up a lot of road room, but not enough for anyone to park, they would easily be able to fit the van in when Jane turned up, by shuffling along a bit.

By two o'clock, Rosie and Jane were ready to leave, and Anna was waiting in her car, now parked further down the road. Suddenly, a car stopped in the middle of the road, unable to find a space and who should get out of it, but Rosie's mother! The woman walked up to the flats and hammered on the door; after a moment a man Rosie didn't know walked up the path too. He appeared to be pulling her mother by the arm, urging her to come away. After calming her, he held her hand and Mildred Wodehouse walked back to his car. Rosie scribbled down the registration make and model and rang Anna.

"Did you see that, Anna?"

"I did. Who is he, Rosie?"

"No idea. But they look very chummy, don't they? Will you do me a favour?"

"I'm on it, I will follow them, besides you will have a slow journey, I'll catch up on the way. Tell you what, stop off the same place we did last time with your dad. I will be on loudspeaker if you need me!"

"You're a star, Anna. See you a bit later, Ciao, darling!" Rosie chuckled. She was pleased her mother hadn't noticed her.

"I don't think you have to be an expert in body language, Rosie. Seems your mother has a man on the go." Jane turned the key. "I'm so sorry."

"I'm not. Gross. Poor Dad. I'm so glad he left her. The woman is a bitch." It was unlike Rosie to speak this way. Bumble hissed and spat, and Bear began barking. The journey would be bedlam.

Jane was certain if ever Walter felt guilty for his actions, Rosie would put him straight about her mother's mystery man. She wouldn't do it otherwise. She had her dad's kind temperament and a breaking point which far outreached most people's.

"Hold on, Jane, let me zoom in a minute." Rosie got some close-up pictures of her mother and the stranger. They were sitting talking in his car, of course they hadn't noticed Rosie in the plain white van or taken any notice of it. One part of her wanted to bang on the car window and give her a piece of her mind. But, as that would no doubt end in a slanging match and prove she wasn't actually in Wales, it might encourage her mother to further visit Bromington.

She felt a gentle touch on her hand. "She isn't worth it, Rosie. If you ever need any help with anything, 'mumsy' then you've got me, you know that."

Rosie felt the sting of tears in her eyes. It wasn't a nice feeling knowing you were never wanted. But it made her feel even more emotional knowing Jane and Anna would never let her down. They'd 'adopted' her between them. The mother and sister she never had were right here now, together with her dad it was all the family she needed.

"Are you finished, Rosie. Shall we go?" Jane asked gently.

Rosie just nodded her head, unable to speak just for a minute. Bear gave her some licks with his small tongue, animals seemed to know how you are feeling.

She cuddled his soft, fluffy fur and remembered to snap a couple of pictures of the home her and Anna were leaving behind. The happiest times of her past.

Anna stayed a couple of cars behind the grey Mini Cooper. Three years old. She was forming a picture in her mind. Working out what sort of a man Mildred was hanging around with. He was quite well-dressed and when they did finally park, she did too. This wasn't the Wodehouse bungalow. Anna had dropped Rosie off there once. No, this was his house. She took her I-pad off the passenger chair and clicked a few pics; close- up's, and she got the man full face. As did she when they kissed. As disturbing as it was, this looked very much like a sexual affair. Yuck.

Anna waited a few minutes then locked her car. She was getting the house number to go with the street. If Rosie wanted to play detective this would give her a bit of a head start.

Rosie had already told her it was in her mind to go through all of Dorothea's papers and personal things they'd taken out of the loft. She wanted to find out everything she could about her dad's family.

Anna was also sure if there was anything untoward going on in Bromington-on-sea following the recent tragedy, Rosie would get the bit between her teeth there too. Although, according to newspaper reports it was nothing more than an accident.

When Anna had told her mum, the body found was one of the two women she'd taken a picture of in the harbour, purely by accident, again, Jane shuddered. She was picking up something before and after the accident. Only she probably wasn't sure what. Maybe when she was in the area, Jane would be more in tune with whatever her gut feeling was telling her.

Someone was re-reading the article, watching with interest how the story was unfolding. Nobody had any idea of what really happened on Sunday evening and maybe they never would. It looked like a clear-cut case, an accident. Which was good. Everyone thought the woman had been alone.

Settling-in period

Two weeks had passed, and the building was transforming itself into a home. Everyone agreed this was their priority for the moment and it was all hands on deck. They really had worked hard as a team. By the end of the week, the Bed & Breakfast was going to be up and running, ready for business.

Rosie had found in the small print from Arkwright & Sullivan Solicitor's that once the initial renovations had taken place, there was to be a monthly allowance for both Rosie at the B & B and Walter at the Garden Centre. A salary, if you will. Also, the estate would cover any outgoings for a five-year period together with staff wages.

Following this time, Dorothea had fully expected both projects to be producing a healthy profit and covering the costs themselves. A projection for this had been calculated and agreed by everyone. Both premises were fully insured for all eventualities and Arkwright Snr. was now able to contribute to both charities as per his instructions after setting aside the final projected amount for Wodehouse residential, B & B and the Garden Centre.

All the staff were kept on at the Garden Centre and Betty, Sybil's sister, was employed at both the B & B in the mornings and a couple of hours a day helping Sybil. Jane and Anna both worked part-time, as did Rosie, all taking turns on a rota system keeping the B & B clean. Betty cooked the breakfasts and they all took bookings, depending who was available.

The outside of the building was brighter, cleaner and sporting full hanging baskets which Walter had put together. He was slowly taking over the planting side of the Centre, while Derek was more of a maintenance man, concentrating on the plant and machinery side. Just like before, Walter was saving his wages, after all, there was nothing he needed. He ran his car which Derek would service from now on, bought the odd piece of clothing and went grocery shopping. By the time the funding stopped he would almost be drawing his pension!

Rosie's pet portrait now had pride of place in her new lounge. The ladies thought of their new homes as 'apartments'. Bumble was now allowed out in the garden without being on Bear's lead. Cats took a while to settle down into a new home. Rosie had the sash window open, the weather was sunny and warm. Just like her friends, Rosie had a few pieces of old furniture mixed in with the new. Dorothea had some lovely things and Rosie, naturally, got first choice. She had the walnut wardrobe and dresser. A French gothic bureau and an antique walnut roll top desk. A heavy ottoman sat at the foot of her bed. Rosie had still not had the time to go through Dorothea's belongings in the basement chest.

Jane was delighted to be given candlestick holders and an art deco style sideboard. Anna was more than happy with the artists easel, which far exceeded the quality of her own. It was a toss-up for the huge free-standing mirror. Anna won! Everything complemented the rest of their furniture in each apartment. A mixture of antique, new and memories.

Bear had a new igloo bed in the corner. He wasn't having any of it. Like before, Rosie had a cat-flap installed in her own kitchen door which serviced both animals and the young pup ran in and out for a good hour every morning before settling on the hearth rug. Bumble favoured the igloo. Most probably because it didn't belong to her. She was also very adept at climbing walls and often sauntered in through Jane's window which was usually left open a few inches. The cat was spoilt for choice.

Rosie was busy with the new Wodehouse Bed & Breakfast menu. Keeping the traditional and mixing in a few other options. Vegetarian, Continental, Full English. Jams and Marmalades from the Garden Centre with a brand-new logo on the jars.

The website was up and running, no longer relying on word of mouth and reputation for trade. They were going to be advertised on booking sites starting the following Monday. The rates were going up, in line with others of the same standard. Rosie was hoping they could earn themselves a few awards too.

Similarly, the Garden Centre now had magnificent pictures of the Bed & Breakfast, together with full-colour brochures. Walter realised they had quite a bit of arable land and was looking to produce a lot more than they did now. A full supply of fruit and vegetables were on the cards. They would make Christmas wreaths and bouquets as well as pre-planted hanging baskets. His gardening expertise was now being put to its full potential.

He had handed over his business in the town to his junior, Justin, together with all his equipment. It was now up to the lad to turn it into a thriving business; he had a good head start and a vast customer list. It was a win-win situation for them all.

Walter was due to meet Rosie tonight. He wanted a chat and the two of them were having supper together. The pearls had been on his mind and he was now feeling a little guilty for leaving his wife high and dry, even if she deserved it. Rosie was going to cook spaghetti, something she'd become used to when she lived on a tight budget. But she rather liked it and Walter found he had a taste for a variety of foods now, most of which he'd been denied for too long.

At seven p.m. Walter tapped on Rosie's window. He'd quickly discovered if he spoke through the intercom, Bear barked for a good fifteen minutes! The buzz from Flat No.1 gained him entry and he pushed the main door. He stepped inside the new bright and airy hallway. The first staircase on the right led up to Jane's floor and the upper staircase led up to Anna's. The interconnecting door locked from this side led to the B & B and another closed door contained the stairs down to the basement. A third door also led into the garden.

"Come in, Dad. I hope you're hungry!"

"Smells delicious, Rosie. Where's Bear?"

"Flat out, snoring on the sofa. He spent all afternoon chasing birds and butterflies in the garden." Walter followed his daughter into the spacious kitchen. She'd laid out places for them both at the dining table.

"What's up, Dad. You're frowning. I know that look!" Rosie placed down two bowls full of spaghetti carbonara and a basket of home-made garlic bread. "Wine?"

"Not if I'm driving..."

"You aren't! The spare room is all made up and the girls might pop around in an hour or so, if that's alright? They've gone out for a pub meal."

Walter ate a few mouthfuls of the delicious chicken and ham in sauce, then laid his cutlery down.

"You're right. There's something on my mind and I wanted to wait until you settled in first."

"Don't tell me you're thinking of leaving, Dad? Surely you aren't going back."

"No, no, it's not that. But I feel guilty. Do you think, Dorothea had good reasons to leave Mildred out of the will?"

"Oh. I'm sure of it. Why do you ask?"

"I had a feeling she would throw away the linens, furs and pearls, but I didn't want her to throw the pearls away. They looked 'real', 'expensive' so, I... I decided to value them."

"And?"

Walter reached into his wallet and took the bill of sale out. He unfolded it and put it on the table.

"What? You *are* joking!"

"No. I made an instant decision, I sold them. Then I went to another jewellers and bought a cheap set. Those are the ones I posted down to your mother."

"Whatever you spent on them, it's more than she deserves," Rosie spat out.

"I can fully understand why you don't like her, after all she's done to you, but..."

"You feel guilty. Leaving her alone, with nothing. The bungalow is in my name. We all have all of this..." Rosie opened her arms wide, "and you think she should be entitled to something, is that it?"

"I know you won't agree with me, but I do feel guilty."

"Dad. I didn't want to show you this, but I will. Meet Audrey." Rosie retrieved a brown envelope from a kitchen drawer and took out several printed photographs. Everything she had taken on her phone and Anna had taken on her I-pad.

Walter turned the photos over, one by one. A frown spread over his forehead and he tapped his fingers on the table.

"She was hammering on my door the day we left London, she never saw us of course. She was with this man, who we now know to be..."

"Arthur. Arthur Green." Walter finished.

"You knew about this?"

"I had no idea. But I know *him*. He's a plumber, came to our place years ago and put in a new bathroom. He also came back and charged me over the odds for new central heating."

"That's not all, Dad. Anna has been doing a bit of digging on social media. Seems Michael has been making a few Australian friends. Mother told you she didn't know the name of Michael's read dad. More lies. It's Fernsby. She has probably made a mistake telling Michael that. He's traced the man, and not only that, he is talking of emigrating. I doubt mother knows too much about that. Michael's been staying at the bungalow now you've gone. Read for yourself."

His conversations didn't make for pretty reading. "Can't wait to get over there; as soon as Mum finds the deeds to this bungalow she's selling up. Starting her own life. I'm getting a big wedge and coming over to Oz!"

That wasn't all. Father and daughter read a catalogue of lies. According to Michael, his sister always was a spoilt bitch, got an inheritance and sodded off. The man he'd lived with all these years was a drunk, a wife beater lived off his dead relatives, never did a day's work and now Michael's mother had chucked him out. She'd found herself a real man.

"Let's pretend I never showed you this receipt, Rosie. Between us we are very well off. First thing next week the bungalow is going on the market. You can sell it and keep the money for your family in the future. One day you'll make a lovely wife and mother. Cheers, darling. I'm looking forward to this evening now!"

It was at this precise moment, Walter and Rosie Wodehouse drew a permanent line between themselves and Mildred Wodehouse and Michael Smith. Walter really couldn't care less what happened to her now. It would be well worth whatever it cost him to get a divorce, on the grounds of adultery. She could move in with her fancy man. And Michael could go to Australia, he never wanted to set eyes on him again. He took his wedding ring off and threw it in the flip-top bin.

"I insist on paying for your divorce out of the proceeds, Dad. And before you hold your hands up in protest, get yourself a new car too. The Jag's never suited you. Get one of those Range Rovers you've always wanted. Treat yourself! We'll split the bungalow money."

"Seventy-thirty in your favour, Rosie. I wonder if Dorothea had any idea about all of this. She hired investigators you know." Walter thought a roomy car was a good idea. He wondered how much of his hard-earned wages had gone in Mildred's, Michael's, or the plumber's direction over the years.

"Seems to me, Dorothea was a very good judge of character, Dad, cheers!"

And so, it was, the Wodehouse apartments were christened that evening. The four friends had their very own housewarming party and plenty of wine. Jane and Walter even did a bit of twisting. Despite all the music and laughter, Bear stayed fast asleep, snoring gently on the end of the huge red comfy sofa. Bumble climbed from Jane's window and jumped to the nearest tree branch. She was off for the night, exploring. She didn't attempt to go up to Anna's level. Sometimes she just arched her back and ran away. Something about Flat No. 3 disturbed her.

The next morning, Walter was working with Rosie, composing a letter to the woman who lived in the bungalow. No longer would she get credence of wife or mother. They were giving her fourteen-days-notice to get out of Rosie's bungalow and take her belongings with her. Her son could get out as well. He also informed her he was issuing divorce proceedings forthwith on the grounds of adultery with one Arthur Green. He had photographic evidence which he would supply if she proved difficult. He bluffed that Dorothea Wodehouse also had further evidence to support his adultery claim, which is why Mildred had not been included in the family will. Her bequeathed gifts were just worthless junk and more than she deserved.

The bungalow was going up for a quick sale and it belonged to Rosalyn Wodehouse. Also, he bluffed, this was written in two generations of wills. It was a family home to pass down the bloodline of Wodehouse members to do with as they pleased. So, it went from Sylvia to Walter to Rosie. Michael said himself, on social media and in the presence of Derek Hawkins, Walter was not his father, and biologically, he wasn't.

That's why she could not find the bungalow deeds, it wasn't hers to sell. Her son, Michael Smith, also to be known as Fernsby, would have to find some other way to fund his emigration to go and live with Fernsby, his real father. Which had been his intention for years. Now the cat would really be among the pigeons with mother and son. Both, untrustworthy and sly individuals. Together with screenshots providing proof of libel, Walter was going in with all guns blazing. He also told Mildred to stay well away from the Garden Centre and Rosie's establishment or they would issue injunctions and restraining orders against her. Walter and Rosie had never felt so complete. Dorothea had injected karma in all their lives.

Rosie begins to unravel matters

A few weeks passed by and despite her insistence of helping in the B & B, Rosie was swiftly over-ruled by Jane and Anna. They both wanted to make the beds, sort the laundry and keep the bathrooms and hallways clean and hoovered. It was not up for debate, they were being paid a part-time wage and wanted to do it. It took them no time at all.

Rosie understood how they felt; it was more a matter of pride. She remembered every time she found groceries how it made her feel. Grateful, but, well, just not nice. With Betty in control of the kitchen, all Rosie had to do was sort out the paperwork. Billing, websites, bookings and all the things she did so well. The tele-sales came in handy now, she had a very patient and professional phone manner. She also updated the Garden Centre, advertising and dragging it into the 21st Century.

Rosie also had a lot of spare time, simply diverting calls to her mobile meant she could go off with Bear on his daily walks. She wasn't tied to the B & B phone. Her dog loved going to the harbour and was quickly making friends with the shopkeepers and villagers.

The bungalow was gone, sold in two weeks flat. Slightly below market price with one of these new internet firms. Michael's Facebook was now set to private. Only Rosie and her father knew of the value of the 'jumble' pearls, the same as only they were privy to how much they both made from the sale of the bungalow. The divorce was not contested, and Rosie thought their bluff about Dorothea having known for some time must have been true. Dad's decree nisi was issued and his divorce would be absolute in six weeks. A good month quicker than Walter had hoped. A top lawyer was worth their weight in gold when you needed one.

Rosie went walking and thinking. Something about the pearls wasn't right. After Dad told her where they had come from, she began to wonder. How had something so valuable found their way onto Judith's stall? Because it seemed she knew very little about them, she just put her hand out and took the money. Rosie had made a point of looking at the jewellery on the stall over the past couple of jumbles which she loved going to with Anna or Jane.

It was nothing special. Certainly not valuable. Mostly it was handmade or sometimes she sold items donated to her, none of it was gold, some of it was silver. There certainly weren't items worth thousands! How had they got in her collection? Rosie would have to tread carefully. She didn't want to ask Judith outright where they came from and draw attention to the matter. Nor would she insult the lady, who may think Rosie was accusing her of something untoward.

It wasn't as if Dorothea did anything wrong. She bought the pearls in good faith. Walter sold them. His wife would have been more likely to bin those as they appeared second-hand.

The more she thought about it, the more likely it seemed Judith had no idea how they got there or what they were worth. £20 was a good sale for her and she took it. Of course, this meant she wasn't exactly honest. The only thing which made any sense was that somebody put them there on the stall for good reason, fully intending to retrieve them. Hiding them in plain view. It was a big risk if someone did that - and then they lost them. Which they did.

Because Dorothea got there first. Would the person have known that or not? Were they watching her, or had they left the building? Why had nobody tried to get them back, or had they? Perhaps the pearls were stolen. If that were the case, Dad would have been in big trouble when he tried to sell them. Her father also knew very little about them when he sold them for a huge sum. The jeweller would have known their true value. Rosie thought it would have been considerably more and very likely the jeweller would have had a buyer waiting. Something didn't add up.

Rosie was also thinking a lot about the accident. Drunk or not you wouldn't step over the fencing near the cliff edge unless you intended on taking your own life, surely? By all accounts, Jennifer showed no signs of depression. In fact, together with her friend they were looking for work, back in the place they had worked before. Dorothea's building. Did they have anything to do with this?

The boat was gone. Lazy Daze had set sail a couple of weeks ago. This time with one couple. According to Barney, Jennifer's husband had moved on. He didn't want to come back to Bromington after he buried his wife. Well, to be precise, he scattered her ashes at sea. He didn't want to come back here at all. Steven Grey was gone. Why did the women give her and Sybil false names? Rosie had a notebook, full of questions.

If Dorothea knew about Rosie's family, what did she know about Nana Wodehouse? She didn't strike Rosie as a vindictive person. She had a sense of humour, yes, a sense of fair play and a generous spirit. There would have been a good reason for her snubbing Sylvia. Rosie was deep in thought about all things.

Rosie's thoughts were interrupted. "Oh, isn't he cute! What's his name?" The fair-haired girl sat down beside Rosie on the bench, calling the small dog to her.

"Be careful! He might snap as he doesn't know you." *Especially as you are more excitable than he is*! "His name is Bear, as you can see, he likes digging!"

"I've seen you here a few times with him. My name's Betsie, I work at the Lobster Pot."

"I'm Rosie, nice to meet you. Are you a local, Betsie?"

"Yes. I've just finished my shift and sometimes it's just nice to sit here for a few minutes. Sorry, I'm not interrupting you, am I? I know, I talk too much!"

If anything, Betsie was just the sort of person who saw a lot of things, but probably didn't pay much attention, Rosie thought.

"No, not at all. I was just sitting here thinking about the accident the other week. Very tragic. It doesn't seem to have stopped people flocking here though. It seems to get very busy as the weather warms up, I've noticed."

"You must be Dorothea's relative. I heard when she was younger, she was very pretty and she had lovely red hair too, just like you. Yes, it was a terrible accident. I think she must have thrown herself off. Why else would you go up there?"

"Suicide? I don't know. Yes. Dorothea was my great aunt. I'm trying to find out a bit about her, we never met."

"You should go to the library then. I'm sure there's local books which will tell you everything you want to now. I had somebody else asking me all about her a few weeks ago."

"Oh, really? That's interesting." Rosie stopped talking, convinced Betsie would just have to tell her.

"Yes, his name was Michael. Funny enough he was down the weekend of the, well, you know, the accident. He asked me if I'd show him the sights, but I don't think that's what he had in mind."

"Did he know Dorothea then?"

"I'm not sure. He was here with his mother, a right misery she was too. She didn't stay more than one night, then booked herself in at the Flag. We did see her during the evening, talking to them women from the boat. She was drunk and abusive. Off her head she was, not all hoity toity like she had been in the morning. Going on about some pearls or something. Made out she'd been left them in some will!"

"Where was this?"

"She was sitting outside the Flag. Michael excused himself, briefly spoke to the women then took his mother up to her room. He told me she was deluded, and did I mind if he walked me home. He'd got a headache. Strange pair altogether. I didn't see him again."

"So, Jennifer, the woman who was found drowned, was still alive at this time then."

"Oh yes, I told the police. Michael was with me then he went back to the Lobster Pot and his mother had gone to bed; oh, it must have been early, before ten o'clock. Then, the next day of course, it was my day off. I didn't know anything about any of it until I came to work Tuesday."

"So, there's no telling how the woman came to be on the cliff edge or what time?"

"No, not really. And so many people were in fancy dress, you wouldn't have known who half of them were. I heard everything got louder and quite rowdy as the night went on. Especially with the fireworks."

"Well, perhaps they were just passing through and heard something about Dorothea along the way. Maybe a tale about a wealthy woman or something!"

"You wouldn't have known it. She didn't spend money, or so I've heard. Hardly left the house the last few years of her life. The very last times was when Sybil or her sister, Betty, drove Dorothea into the village. Mainly to go to the jumble and the bakery. Sometimes for a library book."

"It would have been very unlikely she would have been seen around the village on her own then," Rosie stated.

"No, never. Not in all the years I've worked here anyway. I wouldn't have known what she looked like at all except I saw her once with Sybil. I guessed it was her, nobody else was that old!"

Which means there was no way those two women bumped into Dorothea at the harbour and she happened to mention she needed a cleaner. Especially when she had one anyway.

"Did you know much about the people on the boat then, Betsie?"

"Not a lot. Apparently, they'd been here before but didn't stay long. They were only meant to stay here a short while the second time, then they changed their minds for some reason. That's what my friend, Sue told me. She works in the Flag; on the evening shifts. Very pretty girl, short spiky hair and vivid blue eyes. Nosey she is! Always earwigging when she's meant to be clearing the tables. The four of them used to go in the Flag a lot."

"Perhaps they were millionaires or something idling their days away at sea!"

"Sue thinks they were up to no good. Came across as dodgy, if you know what I mean. Anyway, nice chatting; I'm going home for my tea now, Mum will wonder where I've got to, goodbye Bear! See you again, Rosie."

"Bear!" Rosie cried. "What have you rolled in? Ugh." It was time to go home and get this young scamp in the bath.

"Knock, knock! We've bought cake!" Anna called out. Rosie's front door was open.

"Come in," a voice called out from the bathroom. "Be with you in a minute."

Jane popped the kettle on while Anna took out some side plates. Every Friday the ladies did lunch, usually on the ground floor as it was just easier for Bear to play in the garden while they all nattered.

They had a bit more than cake. Fresh wholemeal rolls, prawns, salad and Marie Rose sauce. Anna chopped and rinsed lettuce and sliced a fresh lemon.

Jane buttered the rolls while the tea brewed. They always worked well together.

A clatter of tiny paws raced towards them and Bear stood in the middle of the kitchen shaking himself from side to side sending drops of water all over the place.

"Oops, sorry! He is being very naughty this morning. Come here, Bear!" Rosie tried to catch him as he ran underneath the table.

"I'm glad I covered the carrot cake!" Jane laughed.

"It's only good clean water. Come here, Bear, see what Auntie Anna has for you!" Her sing song voice enticed the little monkey out and Anna scooped him up once more and wrapped him in his towel.

"We haven't quite finished, young man!" Rosie laughed.

"Could I give him a brush and dry, Rosie? I got him some doggy powder and bits and pieces when he stayed with me." Without waiting for an answer, Jane popped up to her flat and got everything she needed. But first, they had lunch.

Rosie scribbled notes in her pad before she forgot everything Betsie told her. As soon as Bear was perfectly groomed and fluffed up he ran towards the cat-flap. Ah well, at least it was dry outside. Now they could spend time nattering.

"Could I have a look at your pictures for a minute, Rosie?" Jane asked. She flicked through until she found the blown up one of the four with their backs to them. The 'boat people'. "I don't know what it is, but every time I look at them, I have a 'feeling'. You should have told me your mother and brother had been here that weekend. I need the complete picture."

"Sorry, Jane, we didn't want to alarm you any further," Rosie apologised.

"So, according to the barmaid, Betsie, your mother was in bed before ten and your brother was too, both in different hotels. But, not before Mildred mouthed off to people about her pearls. And some time later a woman falls from the cliff top." Anna scratched her head in puzzlement.

"Doesn't seem likely a woman is out with her friends, enjoying a band and then she is so depressed she jumps off a cliff, does it?" Rosie thought the next step should be having a chat with Sue, Betsie's friend. "Anyone fancy a night out?"

Another can of worms

Eight o'clock on Friday evening found the four friends sitting at the bar of the Flag pub. There was no mistaking Sue. She was just as Betsie described her. Rosie had forewarned everyone to be careful in her presence. She was all ears! No, they were there to entice conversation and find out everything they could about the night of the tragedy, not to give anything away. It wasn't too busy in the pub, rather quiet as tomorrow evening the Village Hall was the focal point of the harbour. Which meant no jumble. Both Judith and Miranda who ran the jewellery and fabric stalls were sitting at a corner table; sharing a bottle of wine between them with their evening meal.

Barney, the newsagent and his son, Richard, were playing darts at one end of the pub. Duncan, the harbour master was sitting with a gentleman who had his back to them. If Walter wasn't mistaken, he looked very much like the jeweller who had bought the pearls. The men swiftly finished their drinks and left the pub. Walter waited until Sue was out of earshot before whispering to Rosie. "I just saw Duncan with the manager of Rumbleworth jewellers. No sooner had we sat down, they drunk up and left."

"Are you sure it was him?"

"I was when he turned around to look at me on the way out."

"Two white wine spritzers with lemonade and ice, one port and lemon and an orange juice; anything else?" Sue waited for a reply.

"Peanuts, anyone?" Walter smiled, reaching for his wallet. They must play it cool this evening and let Sue do all the talking, he thought.

"None of us mind walking back if you wanted to have a drink, Walter," Jane offered.

"Thanks all the same, dear, but when I drop you all home, I will be going back to the Garden Centre. We have a large, early morning delivery. I'll be giving Derek and the lads a hand."

"How about tomorrow evening, then? Will you come to the Village Hall? Sounds like fun!" Jane was teasing him, and Walter blushed.

"Are you asking me out?"

"Why not. I'm a modern woman!"

Rosie almost choked, trying to hide a smile while swallowing her wine. Anna raised her eyebrows and the two women shared a knowing glance.

"You should take the lady up on her offer! There isn't too much talent around here," Sue laughed. It didn't go unnoticed she had perched on a stool on the other side of the bar ready to learn all she could about the newcomers.

"Have you lived here long?" Anna dived straight in; they were going to tease it out of her.

"All my life. When we fancy a night out, me and my bestie, Betsie, head off to Bromington Town. There's much more to do there than here. Except if we have one of our special nights - then they all pile down here."

"Like the Glamrocker night?" Rosie asked.

Walter and Jane deliberately began small talk among themselves, showing disinterest in the whole conversation. A ploy they'd just concocted. As Sue wasn't too much younger than their daughters it made sense, they all spoke about the same stuff.

"Yes. Only look how that turned out. I still can't believe it. We already had a few drunks in before the band even started. Even I didn't know a lot of them. They weren't all from these parts."

"We couldn't believe it either; it wasn't a very good start to us moving here!" Anna shook her head at the memory.

"Betsie told me a little about it, we were having a chat earlier. Something about a weird man and his drunken mother and a string of pearls!" Rosie threw that in quickly.

"Oh them. Horrible old woman she was. Rude to me, complained about the food, remarked on my hair and how the tables needed a good wiping. She's lucky I didn't wipe her face with a dirty rag!"

"Sounds like a right old dragon," Rosie smirked.

"She was. Very bitter. Funny enough, the only two people who didn't take any offence by her were those from the boat. One of the men bought a bottle of wine for her and when the band started, she went outside with the women. Just as well, she was already drunk and disorderly. I would have chucked her out, but she was staying here for the night."

"I wonder if the old lady saw anything then. As she was with them, it's all very strange," Anna replied.

"No. I don't think so, according to Betsie this blond-haired bloke she was with, the woman's son, took his mother to her room quite early. No wonder he got a headache, so would anyone having to listen to her going on; she kept on about pearls and fur coats and all other nonsense. Had ideas above her station, I think. Thought she was something she wasn't! She even rang up a few days afterwards, claiming her pearls had been stolen. Daft old bat. Well, I told her they certainly weren't here, our staff aren't thieves."

"What a peculiar woman. You seem to be a good judge of character, Sue. I thought I just saw the harbour master sitting over there, doesn't he patrol the area?" Rosie thought a bit of flattery would work well here.

"Duncan? Well, supposedly. Didn't do a good job that night though, did he? They need a few warning signs up on those cliff edges. I've always said it."

"Was he one of the two men who just left?" Walter piped up. "I've been meaning to find out about fishing permits in the area and sea fishing."

"Yes, the one who was facing this way, that was Duncan. He was sitting with his brother-in-law, Ivan. Not that he has anything to do with the harbour! He owns an exclusive jewellers, just the place for a fancy ring. Know what I mean!"

Sue gave a saucy wink and went off to fill up the ice bucket.

"Do you use the local hairdresser's, Sue? I could do with a bit of a restyle myself," Anna asked, when Sue returned.

"I have a card here, tell them I sent you and you'll get a 10% discount! Ask for Izzy if you want something outrageous. If you want more of a, well... traditional cut, try Sandra."

"Do they cut men too? I saw it was unisex and I need a bit of a trim!"

"Why don't you take your new girlfriend too? You can have a family day out!" Sue burst out laughing.

Now it was Jane's turn to blush. From the neck upwards. Sue was a bit of a character; it probably went with the job. Everyone turned to the door as a group of four tourists walked in, at least that's what Sue guessed they were. Once she was out of earshot they began to whisper.

"I don't think I'm ready for blue, purple and blonde, although a fairytale unicorn resemblance does suit Sue. I am thinking of a total restyle. What do you say we try and get booked in tomorrow, Rosie? Prepare ourselves for the local barn dance!"

"I'm happy to go with Sandra. My hair needs thinning out and I have a few split ends," Rosie agreed.

"If none of you mind, can we just have one more drink and save ourselves for tomorrow evening?" Jane suggested.

"Good idea, Mum. In fact, we can always leave now if you like. I have a new face mask and a good book to catch up on," Anna said.

Walter shrugged, he was easy either way, but he did have a lot to do tomorrow. An early night would be good.

"Fine by me. Bear told me I'm only allowed out once a week." They all laughed at Rosie and took the opportunity to escape while Sue was taking an order to the kitchen. They had enough info for one night.

Rosie asked her dad in for a cup of tea before he drove home, and the other two ladies went to their own apartments.

They all knew when it was group time or private time. They were that tuned in with each other.

Apart from a chewed slipper, Bear had been a good boy. He was even sound asleep inside his igloo. Rosie thought he probably felt safe in there when he was alone. Well, he wasn't quite alone. His head was resting on the floppy fur bunny Anna kindly donated. Mr. Bugs was a comforter she no longer needed!

"I'm scribbling more notes, Dad. The stuff Sue told us this evening was very interesting!"

"I'm beginning to think Dorothea had a lucky escape, Rosie. The bunch from Lazy Daze took an interest in Mildred. They had wormed their way in this house, or at least the ladies did, and they were trying to come back again when you took over."

"Looking for something, perhaps? If that was the case then there's only one conclusion, Dad. The expensive pearls belonged to them."

"Exactly. And why dump them in the jumble? Obviously, it was only temporary, they fully intended to retrieve them after..."

"After what? What reason would they have to take them off their boat?"

"Customs and excise?"

"And don't you think it's convenient, Dad, the very man who is meant to guard the harbour failed miserably on the night of the 'death' and just happens to be related to a jeweller?"

"Quite so. But, here's the thing; if Duncan, the harbour master and his brother-in-law, Ivan, were in some sort of dodgy business regarding the pearls, how did they know I'd eventually decide to sell them and bring them to that particular jeweller?"

"Why did you? Suddenly decide to sell them I mean?"

"Maybe it's because I kept seeing this advert. It was placed in the newsagent's window. Best prices paid for top quality jewellery. I jotted down the number. I saw the flyer inside the Village Hall saying the same thing. When Nigel, the security man was reading the local paper I saw a half page advert for the same jewellers; maybe I was getting one of these subliminal messages. I've no idea! I was originally intending just getting them valued, as I've told you. I had a feeling they might be valuable."

"Did Sybil know the content of Dorothea's will, do you think, before we did?"

"Oh, without a doubt. She was her best friend and confidante. Remember, she helped her buy the 'worthless' pieces for Mildred. I think it was a bit of a joke on their part. Knowing what they did about Mildred and Arthur. Fur coat and no knickers, isn't that the saying?"

"I believe it is, Dad. Yet both Sybil and Derek had the common decency not to tell you about the affair. But, in all innocence, Sybil or Betty or any number of people could have indulged in a little gossip about the pearls and stuff. Rumours are easily spread."

"I think we may have the bare bones of something here. Duncan could have started a rumour about some sort of a check, even if there wasn't, he must have been in with the smugglers or thieves or whatever the boat people were and talked them into temporarily hiding the pearls."

"Maybe. I don't know what their intentions were, who they were going to sell them to, but Duncan probably told them they couldn't sell the pearls through conventional channels, meaning high-street jewellers. Convincing them the only safe way would be through Ivan. Maybe they had a regular scam going. Who knows?"

"Yes, Rosie, and probably Duncan and Ivan have connections and intended to make bundles of money themselves this time. We don't know if Duncan even suggested placing the pearls on the jumble table because he had a mystery shopper in place, only Dorothea thwarted his plans, she got in there first!"

"And if there was gossip afterwards, Duncan may well have found out Dorothea was leaving the pearls in her will."

"Next... they would simply wait for the recipient to collect them and then jump in with a very generous offer. Meanwhile, the boat people talked their way into Dorothea's home posing as cleaners while really searching for their booty!"

"Which they didn't find, because Sybil had them the whole time."

"And then I come along and made the job a whole lot easier. By walking into the very jewellers who have been patiently waiting for my soon to be ex-wife to collect what was hers."

"No wonder you didn't have to try too hard to sell them on. And I've a feeling this is all connected to Jennifer Grey's death, which may have been murder."

"Which has everything to do with Mildred shouting about being bequeathed pearls in a drunken state."

"The boat people cannot have known you sold the real pearls *before* Mother's visit. Duncan and Ivan must have double-crossed them. They honestly believed Mildred had been given the genuine, original inheritance. Which is why they plied her with wine, intending to rob her perhaps."

"I think we need to start crossing people off your possible murderer suspect list, Rosie. Sybil, Betty and Derek are first off. They sat with something so valuable for months, making no attempt to have it valued. They are of better character than I am!"

"So, we just have Jennifer's husband Steven, Sandra and Jack.

Duncan, Ivan and whoever they sold the pearls on to, had no reason to murder anyone, they already knew the truth. Mother did not have the genuine pearls. They would not have been involved in trying to retrieve what they probably guessed were just cheap replacements. They weren't even at the Flag on that Sunday night, I don't think. Sue never mentioned them."

"Don't forget your mother was on the scene, as was Michael. We only have a barmaid's word they were both in bed early."

"Hmm, they might be a lot of things, but I don't have them down as murderers! There could have been plenty of others within earshot outside the Flag? The pretty dumb boat people could have easily said the pearls were worth a fortune."

"You're right, Rosie. If the boat people were stupid enough to leave precious pearls the way they did, who knows what happened that night. If Mildred was that drunk, they could easily have taken the pearls out of her bag if she was carrying them. Or someone else; how that led to a death - I'm not sure yet."

"We are making a lot of guesses. But we do know Mother came here with her pearls and went home without them. Someone robbed her, thinking she had something very valuable."

"If it was the boat people, they would have seen the difference. But we do know something isn't right, don't we?"

"I'm just a little concerned you might be involved in something dishonest, Dad. Unwittingly, of course."

"Don't worry yourself about that. I've a feeling the pearls are long gone, and any paperwork trails probably don't exist. I also think they were worth a lot more than I was paid for them. These sort of transactions, probably don't go 'through the books.' Let's have another look." Walter took the bill of sale out of his wallet again. "500000 in small print it says IR. Neither does it mention pearls. It just says miscellaneous."

"Curious. How did they pay you?"

"My bank statement just said international credit."

"In a way you ended up being a middleman in something corrupt, Dad. Maybe we should pay a little visit to that jewellers on Monday?"

"Let's give it a bit of thought. There are a few other people, involved in this, Rosie. Judith, who sold the pearls. Dorothea, who bought them, even though she's departed, it could have a comeback on her businesses; you, Anna, Jane. Sybil could be classed as an accomplice! Derek as another accomplice, fencing stolen goods, or words to that effect!"

"And it is an awful lot of money to lose if we're working on a hunch, Dad."

"It could be an insurance scam for all we know. Something of that nature. Why, the pearls could even be back from where they originated. In another form, bracelets, earrings. Who knows?"

"So, for now, we should just concentrate on what happened to Judith and why."

Saturday night

Anna was on the phone first thing. "You do? That's great, okay then. We'll see you at two-thirty."

"Would you mind if we popped into Bromington Town for an hour this morning first, Anna? I'd like to get something new for tonight," Rosie asked.

"I tell you what, how about we park up and go off on our own for a couple of hours. We have totally different clothes tastes and I was going to buy a few things too."

"Sounds great." It was perfect; actually. Rosie had found Rumbleworth jewellers online and was determined to pay a visit. She wanted to browse around and see if the pearls were for sale and for how much.

There was only one problem with that when she got there. The jewellers wasn't. The only thing she saw in the window was a 'To Let' sign. Rumbleworth's and Ivan had gone. There was no 'new premises' notice. She exhaled, only then realising she had been holding her breath. This was a good thing. She had tossed and turned last night worrying for her dad.

No shop, no pearls, no records. Apart from his bank balance. There *was* that. Even so, she knew it was playing on his conscience. This news might ease his troubled mind a bit. At least on the plus side, her mother had no idea her husband had double-crossed her, and she never would. Only Rosie and Walter knew about that. So, where were the cheap pearls? Maybe if Rosie could find those, she'd find the potential murderer. The police had made some sort of a mistake. Jane also 'felt' it strongly. Something was off.

There were not going to be answers this end. Just how well did Sybil and Derek know Duncan the harbour master? Perhaps she could wheedle some information tonight. In fact, while everyone else was letting their hair down, Rosie thought it would be a great time to start asking questions. Most people were more truthful after a touch of alcohol.

She felt a tug on her arm and spun around.

"Wow! you're jumpy! We've just got time for lunch you know. I'm looking forward to a new hairdo, luxury bath and a bit of fun!" Anna was buzzing.

"Sorry, I was miles away. I was thinking, tonight could be perfect for finding out bits and pieces, odds and ends. The hall will be packed with locals." Rosie had bought something very special for Jane, who was once again 'Bear sitting'. "Do you think your mum will like this?"

"Wow, she's going to love that, it's beautiful. Where did you find it?"

"In a lovely little shop tucked away on the outskirts of town. 'Let Bygones be Bygones'. *Antique Art Nouveau Sterling Silver Filigree Bezel Set Blue Glass Bracelet.* The slip of paper said inside the box. I hope it has good vibrations because all the best things are used! I also have something for you, Anna."

"Oh, you shouldn't have. What is it?" Anna laughed. She was clapping her hands like an excited child.

"Not here. You will have to wait until you get home. Special delivery this morning!"

"Oh, you tease. Just for that it's your turn to buy the cake. Red velvet with a side order of iced coffee!"

"You're on! I even managed to find something special to wear tonight. But I'm keeping it under wraps!"

"Well, Boo-boo, I won't share my finds either. Sue was right, they do have some amazing shops here. Talent's not too bad either. You must check out the hardware shop; wow! I almost went in to buy something or another just to get served by the hunk in the tight jeans. Actually, scrap that; he's mine!"

Rosie laughed. "Sounds like he walked straight out of a launderette advert rubbing his wet coke can over his chest! No, give me an intellectual man any day of the week. You're welcome to mister all brawn and no brains!"

With a sharp dig to her ribs, Rosie yelped and then chased after her playful friend who could always outrun her. They felt like they'd been friends forever. Hopefully by now the kind delivery men would have arrived and Anna's surprise should be waiting in her apartment.

"Hello, Rosie. Pleased to meet you, I'm Sandra. Wow! I love your red hair, look at your curls. I think I have just the thing for you; why don't you look at these styles."

"Thank you." Rosie held the folder in both hands and began to browse. Part of her was thinking of a total restyle; something a lot shorter, a far more manageable cut. Presently, her hair was almost as wide as it was long and then something caught her eye.

"Can you make me look like this?" Rosie found a model with a striking cut which was only two inches below her jaw at the front and cropped slightly higher at the back. The long curls just parted on one side of her head.

"I can do better than that, because your hair is so much nicer. How about a few lowlights to soften the look?"

"I'm all yours," Rosie smiled. For too many years she'd chopped her own hair, mostly due to a lack of funds. The new style would go so well with her new outfit. White jeans, tassled ankle boots, a chiffon blouse over a plain white vest tee-shirt. Now her new necklace with the small chain drop at the back would be visible!

Not to be outdone, Anna was going for a chic short hairstyle. Totally cut in at the back with a defined straight edge no longer than a number two razor cut, while the remainder of her hair was being cut layer upon layer upon layer. Short enough one side to tuck behind her ear while the other half flopped down to her chin. She was having just the slightest dip of dark blue teased through the ends of her dark shiny hair.

Luckily there were other stylists because Walter was dropping in around 4.30 for a quick snip.

Rosie didn't ask any questions that afternoon, she was saving them all for later. This was the calmest she had felt for months. Waves of contentment and relaxation enveloped her. Betty was a godsend, as three rooms in the B & B were booked tonight. Jane always left a small vase with a few freshly cut flowers from the garden in every room. The red roses were fragrant and stylish, and these small touches were getting them great reviews.

"So, how's it all going up at Wodehouse? Are you all settling in alright?" Sandra asked while she wrapped small strands of Rosie's hair in foils.

"Perfect. We've had a few alterations made inside and out. Business is booming. It sure beats my last job," Rosie laughed.

"That's what it's all about. Me and Izzy have been friends since college and one day we were determined to have our own salon. We've even got a flat upstairs."

"Don't be bashful, Sandra. Just be honest!" Izzy interrupted. Rosie could see in the mirror her tongue was slightly to one side as she chewed her lip, deep in concentration with the precise cutting of Anna's straight hair.

"Ha! Okay, Izzy is my partner. She's the butch one. You'd never have guessed, would you?"

The fact Izzy has a buzz cut, rainbow dm's and two nose piercings, while you have flouncy locks, a shortish flowing dress and flowery sandals does sort of indicate that. "Not really, no, well - maybe just a little," Rosie fibbed.

"Are you both going to the Village Hall tonight?" Anna asked.

"Sometimes we do, it isn't really our scene though. If we go out in town, we have friends in the gay bars who aren't so, well, how can I put it?" Izzy laughed.

"Christian?" Anna replied.

"Something like that," Sandra said.

"The older generations aren't always so liberal with their thinking," Izzy grumbled.

"Well, we're going, so if you change your mind, pop along. My mum, Jane, will be there too. Bit of an old hippy, a sensitive and very liberal. She has an LGBT sticker in her van just to be controversial."

"My dad, Walter, will be there as well. When he's had a few bitters, he will probably let his hair down and do his dad dancing!"

The hairdressers laughed. "I think your dad might be booked in for a cut later; the name Walter rings a bell," Sandra smiled.

"It was quite shocking what happened a couple of months ago, wasn't it?" Anna suddenly announced.

Sandra and Izzy gave each other a look. It wasn't for Izzy to say, so she left it to her girlfriend.

Sandra looked around before lowering her voice to a hushed whisper. "We think there was something a little odd about all of that."

"Really?" Rosie was all ears.

"It was all to do with her scar, skin tag, or whatever it was," Sandra faltered.

"Who?" Anna asked.

"The woman they found in the sea, Jennifer Grey. She came in here three times during two stays at the harbour. I always cut her hair. Well... the first time it was there. The second time it wasn't and the third time it was back again."

"You've lost me!" Rosie said, sipping at her coffee.

"I noticed the first time I cut her hair she had this, whatever it was at the back of her head. I felt it when I gave her a shampoo and was mindful when I gave her a cut. On the second visit it wasn't there, which I thought was odd, but of course, I didn't say anything, it would be rude. So, imagine how shocked I was when she came back again, and it was there. The same as the first time."

"There was only once conclusion I could think of," Izzy said. "Stands to reason, it wasn't the same person, there was two of them."

"Twins?" Anna asked, puzzled.

"That's what we think. But that's why it's odd. We only ever saw one woman. That wasn't all of it, her friend, Sandra popped in the second time Jennifer was having her hair done and called out: 'Just popping to town Jan, see you a bit later'."

"Are you sure she didn't say Jen?" Anna asked.

"Quite sure," Sandra replied.

Rosie thought back to the Village Hall that day. Janice and Helen, they'd called themselves. All of Rosie's niggling doubts now became a solid bona fide theory.

"As we're all being honest, we think something is afoot too. When I first came here, they approached me and Sybil at the jumble, asking for work at the house. They said they'd been cleaners there for a few weeks before Dorothea died. One said her name was Helen the other called herself Janice."

"Thank you, Rosie! I *knew* it, Izzy. I told you didn't I! We don't have any choice now do we. We must tell the police. If there was two identical women and only one was ever seen at any one time, then where has the other one disappeared to?" Sandra was getting in a bit of a flap.

Rosie's stomach did a flip. If the police became involved and they had to confess all about the pearls, then what? Maybe it wouldn't come to that if they could be a little bit vague about that point. It was no use; best her and Dad came clean tomorrow with Anna and Jane. Jane, who did have a good legal friend, could maybe find out where the land lay. Rosie had been thinking earlier, that maybe her dad could put a chunk of the money to good use in the local community. A new church roof for a start. She was panicking.

"Let's at least wait until tomorrow. I will talk to Dad about it and Jane. There's a few more points we will need to speak to them about. Is that okay, Sandra?"

"Yes. I understand that my piece of information, now it's added to yours, warrants a genuine concern."

They arrived at the Village Hall at 7.30 that evening in good time to save seats.

Izzy and Sandra were already sitting at a long table, quite alone. A few other villagers had made a point of squashing together elsewhere.

"Are these seats taken?" Anna winked.

"Not at all, help yourselves!" Izzy grinned.

"You've met Rosie's dad, this is my mum, Jane."

Jane immediately offered her hand to the couple. Nobody had to bother to tell her they were together. She knew. "Well, you can only be the very talented scissor ladies. You have transformed my already beautiful girls into princesses!"

"Let's save three of these chairs for Sybil, Betty and Derek." Rosie plonked some of the bags full of booze and snacks on the spare seats.

"I'll show you where the kitchen is, you can get glasses in there." Sandra stood and Jane and Walter followed her.

"Your mum rocks, and she is a beauty, just like you, Anna!" Izzy laughed. "Don't worry, I'm not hitting on you, just in case you were hoping!" Izzy was impressed at Jane's turn of phrase. Just one word away from scissor sisters, something all the frumps just wouldn't understand.

"I'm glad we've got that out of the way, Izzy. I was rather hoping to see a certain person here tonight; he works in the town. A muscular hunky male all biceps and triceps."

"What about you, Rosie? Any special type?"

"She's on the look-out for a Hercule Poirot minded sort, just twenty-five years younger, without the moustache!"

"Then you might be in luck, Rosie Wodehouse. In fact, the local plod has just walked in, he always comes here in an off-duty capacity, but just to keep an eye out the club shuts on time. Barney doesn't always lock up promptly otherwise!"

All eyes turned towards Matthew Walker. Rosie's lingered a few seconds longer than everyone else's.

"Not my type," whispered Anna. Only because she could see her best friend's eyes were on stalks. He was drop dead gorgeous as it happens. In a policeman sort of way. Short brown shaved hair with a bit of a quiff on the top. Athletic build, shirt sleeves rolled up a couple of times and it least the bottom wasn't tucked into his waistband, that would have been a no-no.

Anna turned away and chatted with Izzy about all the single men in the vicinity. Both her and Rosie looked lovely tonight, they had scrubbed up well, as had their parents. Jane was wearing her brand-new bracelet and Anna had felt like all her Christmases had come at once when she went home just after four o'clock that day.

Rosie had always wanted to return a gift ever since Anna had painted Bear and Bumble. Her best friend was now the proud owner of a brand-new palette. Oils, the finest brushes and canvases she'd ever owned. It was Rosie's way of paying her back for all the teabags, milk, packets of cereal and other substance foods she'd slipped her over the last three years too.

Not only that, Rosie had generously paid for both their hairdo's and tipped the ladies well.

"Let me help you with those," Matthew offered, taking the glasses out of Jane's hands.

"That's very kind. Won't you join us? Shove along, Rosie." If ever a woman was as astute as Jane, she would do well in life. Just one look at the young man and she'd known which young lady would have been his type.

Rosie cringed and Anna smirked. *Subtle mother, very subtle!*

"I don't want to intrude on your table, but I'm here alone, so why not! Rosie, I'm Matthew, nice to meet you."

Within thirty minutes the Village Hall was very packed. The band was just about to begin and in walked Anna's dream man from the hardware shop. On his own. Could the night possibly get any better?

Yes, it could. Even Betty had a companion and the couples danced the night away. Anna, who had had a few drinks, made a beeline for the shop assistant, who it turned out was called Brandon. It was in fact his hardware shop.

Sybil confessed she may have told a few close friends about Dorothea's will, including Duncan the harbour master when he came to the café. Derek serviced his car for him, and they were quite good friends. They were all intrigued about the Wodehouse family before they arrived and yes, Duncan had thought it funny regarding the furs and pearls. In fact, he'd said if she doesn't like the jumble pearls send her along to my brother-in-law, Ivan. He'll give her a bad price for them, it was a bit of a joke among them.

In fact, he did know Derek and Sybil were keeping them safe at the Garden Centre. He did say, Sybil remembered, if she doesn't come for them, don't give them to charity, Ivan will give you more, a very fair price. I'm sure Dorothea would rather you benefitted from them if that was the case.

Rosie thought that was very valid information. The boat people were not looking for the pearls there, no, just at the house, which Duncan knew all too well. She didn't remember much more about Saturday night, apart from lots of dancing, and Matthew walking her home.

Matthew was the perfect gentleman and stopped Rosie tripping over a few times by linking her arm through his. They had such a great night together, it was just a shame that being swept up with the atmosphere his new lady friend was a little worse for wear.

He felt like he'd known her for years. She made him laugh and he loved the way the small dimple appeared in her cheek when she laughed. Right now she was singing a few tunes the band had played and he wouldn't dream of recording her! Not that she couldn't hold a tune, mostly because she had forgotten the words and was repeating the same lines.

Some way behind them he could hear Rosie's friend, Anna, making just as much noise, if not more, with her escort. The evening had gone over time, but not by much. The atmosphere was highly charged and the newcomers to Bromington had injected much needed life into the proceedings.

"Matthew, Matty, Matty, Matthew, I love you," Rosie giggled. Then she launched into another song, clutching his arm tightly.

"Soon be there, Rosie. I will see you inside and make you a nice hot drink before I go home."

"Don't forget the biscuits. Cake, cake will be better. Help yourself won't you? Bear likes cake, but Bumble is fussy. I like cake, I like wine too. We had fun, didn't we, Matthew?"

Rosie looked up, pecked him on the cheek and carried on with another tune.

Sunday afternoon

Rosie's eyes opened and she blinked a few times. Somewhere in the distance, Bear was barking his head off. She sat up slowly and surveyed her room. Bumble was asleep at the foot of the bed. Like a guardian. She was happy to see her new blouse hanging up even if her jeans were on the floor. The black smudge on her pillowcase a messy sign she hadn't quite managed to take her make-up off the night before. Ah well, who cares! Sunday's were meant for a nice lay in! Memories of the evening came flooding back to her. Matthew was really nice and didn't seem at all like a policeman, let alone a sergeant. Not that she'd ever come up that close and personal before. They had danced very well together, fast, slow and everything in between; they'd laughed, joked and made a promise to meet today at... goodness! In thirty minutes. She jumped out of bed.

Aside from having a shower, picking up her clothes and feeding her hungry pets, Rosie was in a right tizzy. She was convinced she didn't look anywhere near as attractive as she had last night. The buzzer rang and she turned from the bed to the mirror to the window, not knowing which way to turn. Bear duly began barking continuously and it was bedlam. The buzzer rang again. "Coming," she called out, then hurriedly pressed the intercom.

"Dad! Matthew! Sybil! What are you all doing here?"

"Noon, you said, at your flat. Although at this point, Matthew is not here in an official manner," Sybil smiled.

"And before you say a word, I've been talking with your father on the way home last night. I do believe I may have accidentally sent your mother the wrong pearls and the wrong linens. The furs were the only ones, Dorothea couldn't have muddled those. So, the other set of pearls were left here, at this house, also the French linens, which were the remainder of the estate, which was all bequeathed to you, Rosie. Just to be clear. They were yours to sell or do with as you pleased. Dorothea bought them in good faith. I was with her - and Judith sold them in good faith. It's the others who haven't been so honest."

Rosie stood with her mouth agape. It would seem her and Walter had just been given a good enough reason to come clean about everything and explain all to Matthew.

"Please, come in. Excuse the mess, and me; I overslept."

Matthew gave her a huge smile with his mouth and his eyes. "You look fine, now whatever is this all about?"

"Can I just go and get Anna and Jane, because they don't know all of it." Rosie ran upstairs and woke her friends.

Jane was as fresh as a daisy, but it appeared Anna had company. "It isn't what it looks like," she whispered through the gap in the door. "He slept on the sofa he couldn't drive last night."

"Hey, you don't have to explain anything to me. Rain check?"

"Yes, please."

"I will fill you in later, have fun!" Rosie didn't judge, but her friend didn't lie. If she said he fell asleep on the sofa, then he probably did. In his tight jeans.

The five of them sat around the kitchen table drinking tea or coffee. Rosie had her pages of scribbled notes and she began to relay her story. If Sybil had any doubt Rosie might incriminate herself or Walter she quickly butted in, they were only small fibs about the pearls. A slight twisting of the truth, none of it mattered anyway. Mildred had thrown two things straight in the bin and lost her cheap pearls. The only thing Walter felt guilty about was the amount he had been paid for them and hoped Sybil and Derek wouldn't hold it against him. They didn't. Everybody knew in the long run he wouldn't have spent the money on himself. Although he had indulged in a new car, but that was out of the bungalow money.

Matthew had a good nose for criminals, and there were none sitting in front of him today. He was also aware of porkies but chose to turn a blind eye. Once Rosie had relayed practically her whole life story, he had a very clear picture of Mildred Wodehouse. If he was honest, he would probably have done the same thing.

"Let me run through this, just to be clear," Matthew said. He wasn't writing notes, this wasn't a formal statement, not at all.

"Dorothea Wodehouse left you the Garden Centre, Walter, and left you this building and the remainder of her estate, Rosie. She left Mildred some furs, linens and pearls, which may or may not have got muddled along the way.

Sybil posted the items down to Mildred who had flatly refused to come to Bromington, except when she arrived with her son with the sole intention of becoming a nuisance and causing trouble. You since found out that your wife had been having an affair for years, something Dorothea was well-aware of, hence the cheap items she bequeathed her. You filed for a divorce which will be final soon. Your wife and son came to Bromington on the weekend of the tragic accident, which you don't believe was an accident at all. During this time, Mildred Wodehouse was drunk and disorderly and told a number of people, including the four from Lazy Daze she had about her person, pearls, which had been bequeathed to her. That same evening, Jennifer Grey fell to her death on the edge of the cliffs.

The women had approached you in the Village Hall, having got themselves work at this building, which Sybil knew nothing about. At this point they called themselves Helen and Janice. You now believe they planted valuable stolen pearls on the jewellery stall, probably under instruction of the harbour master, Duncan, brother-in-law to Ivan of Rumbleworth jewellers, which has since closed. You sold them for £500,000 at the jewellers. Dorothea bought them for £20 from an unsuspecting Judith. Both women were innocent, as were you, when you originally went to the jewellers to value them, believing them to have belonged to Dorothea and passed down to Rosie. Neither Dorothea, Judith, Sybil or yourself, were aware these were very possibly stolen goods."

At this point, both Rosie and Walter looked at the floor. If this was the way it was going to pan out with Sybil's help, so be it. Two sets of pearls; accidentally swapped by Dorothea. No mention of Walter buying any from another jeweller.

"Sounds about right so far, Sergeant Walker. That's why I'm here, because I know more about what went on before these dear people arrived," Sybil smiled. "What with Dorothea's absent-mindedness of course. She kept most of her valuable stuff in the locked chest. Which, if I recollect, she may very well have muddled the linens and pearls inside and given me the wrong things to look after."

Matthew raised his eyebrows at the tall tale.

"And Rosie, you believed it wasn't the case this woman asking you for work was depressed?"

"Exactly. Not at all. They came across as shifty. Obviously, they were less than honest. Betsie told me she had only seen Dorothea once in the harbour in the months before she died.

That was the day she was with Sybil at the jumble. There is no way she was walking around on her own asking complete strangers if they would like cleaning jobs."

"Not in a million years," Sybil interrupted. "I don't even know what day of the week they came cleaning here, Betty did three days a week, they must have known that somehow and turned up another day. Dorothea wouldn't have known she'd even asked them in during the last few weeks, she was a bit scatty by then."

"It stands to reason, they were here every week looking for the pearls, probably pinching things too, I wouldn't be surprised," Jane added.

"While all along... Duncan, if he was responsible for making the boat people plant the pearls at the jumble, knew they were in your possession, Sybil?"

"Yes. Only we had security camera's see. Not as good as the ones we have now, but enough to give evidence, Duncan knew that. He would know and so would Ivan, exactly where the pearls were at any time. They were biding their time, see what panned out, if they *were* stolen it probably made sense to leave it a while."

"Only of course, Sybil, they were rubbish; the ones you had, were just cheap. All along, the jumble pearls were locked in a chest, which Rosie found in the loft when she moved in."

"Yes. All very confusing isn't it, Matthew? Shall we get to the point then." Sybil was getting a little flustered with her white lies.

"The points being then:

If all of this is true and some sort of smuggling was going on and this might not have been the first time, it was a joint effort between the boat people, Duncan the harbour master and his brother-in-law, Ivan, who just happens to have closed shop and gone. Only this time they hatched a plan to cut the boat people out and take the money themselves. Very probably the pearls were worth many times more than they gave Walter.

Dorothea throws a spanner in the works by grabbing the pearls as they were the closest thing to her on the jewellery stall. Sybil confirms to Duncan that her and Derek have the pearls at the Garden Centre. He used his position as a family friend to find out what he wanted to know, the whereabouts of the gems. He wasn't to know they were a cheap set which were later posted down as instructed, from Walter to Mildred.

Meanwhile, Walter and Rosie find the jumble pearls in the trunk with everything else bequeathed to Rosie; after valuing them, Walter sells, naturally. So, he has just taken to Ivan, the main nearby jeweller, what it was Ivan and Duncan have been waiting for. Of course, still not knowing what he's sold. By pure fluke their prize unexpectedly arrives.

When Mildred arrives in town telling everyone and especially the boat people about her pearls, they can't believe their luck. Obviously, they want to retrieve them, not knowing they are a different set of cheap pearls, and upcoming events lead to a death.

Now, according to the hairdresser, Jennifer Grey has an identical twin. One has a distinctive mark on her head, like a large skin tag and the other doesn't. I'm guessing Jennifer did, as she was the one who went to the hairdresser on occasions one and three and Janice went on occasion two, confirmed by Sandra Hughes popping her head in the salon and calling her Jan."

"I think that's all of it, Matthew," Rosie nodded.

"Off the record, it seems you are all innocent in any of this if it turns out to be the truth. Without a picture of the pearls we will have to check the records to find out if there have been any cases over the last few months of a burglary with anything of that value. I wouldn't go spending anymore of the cash for now, Walter. If there has been a burglary and we can tie this all up then you may be in for a substantial 10% reward for assisting in the case. Which would more than cover your new car and give you plenty spare!

If there hasn't been a reported case, well, then I can't see there's any way you would have to pay anything back. The pearls were purchased fairly and squarely. No doubt you would generously reward Judith, Sybil and maybe the church."

"On the record?" Sybil asked.

"On the record, we shall have to open up the case again. Trace those from the boat, we only had the husband's word as official identification. We need to find that boat, I hope it's not somewhere we have no jurisdiction. Plus of course, we must find out exactly where Ivan is and pull in Duncan for questioning. We will need an address for your mother, Rosie, if you have one, and take her and her son in for questioning."

"Phew! This is such a relief, it was only yesterday after speaking with Sandra at the hairdressers that everything began to tie in, between her and myself. And then I was worried we'd done something wrong."

"Not the way I see it. Maybe you can just refresh your memories a little about the jumbled pearls, just so you all remember it the same way. We shall be back in an official capacity. But not today, maybe I will bring a constable with me tomorrow and we can take a few statements from you. Not you, Jane. You were in London when all of this happened, and as I understand it, Anna doesn't need to be involved either. She has nothing to contribute to the pearl story."

"This is the receipt for the pearls, by the way," Walter handed it over.

"500,000 IR. Hmm. International payment? You were right to have suspicions. Keep hold of it for now."

"The problem is, Matthew, Jennifer's husband had her cremated and threw the ashes away at sea," Rosie said.

"The only way we will know who he identified is to find the twin sister, if there is one. I'm going back to the office to get onto this right away. Thank you everyone, for your help. Will you ask Sandra to come here tomorrow morning, about eleven o'clock? We will arrive in a plain car, we don't want your guests to think you're up to no good."

"I'll see you out, Matthew." Rosie shut the door and walked outside. "Look, I'm really sorry. I told Sandra yesterday afternoon we'd come to the Police Station and give you the full story. I don't even remember blurting it all out last night."

"You didn't, well, not all of it. A slightly different account to Sybil's today. Just a little matter of the muddled pearls. For what it's worth, if she was my mother... well... If you don't mind me asking, what are you doing Tuesday evening?"

"Cooking a delicious meal for two I believe."

"Sounds perfect, and what time would this be?"

"How about six-thirty going on for seven? Is there anything you don't like?"

"About you? No."

Matthew leaned forward and very gently brushed his lips against Rosie's. "See you tomorrow. Oh, and by the way, I walked you home safely last night, and no, I didn't come in, just so you know!"

Rosie found herself blushing. Had she asked him to, or was he just teasing. He glanced around and smiled. A girl could be forgiven if she had. Rosie went back inside her flat.

"Oh, come on now; don't be silly, Walter. It's none of our business and no, we don't think you're a bad person!" Sybil scolded.

"She's right, Mr. Wodehouse. Why would anyone give a string of pearls to an adulterous witch if they were worth a small fortune? Besides, it would have made your poor Aunt Dorothea turn in her grave," Jane agreed.

"Besides the point, Jane. I didn't know at the time she was having an affair," Walter sighed.

"No, but you did soon afterwards, Dad. Sybil and Jane are right, and Matthew is turning a blind eye to that part. Sybil is quite correct, Dorothea left me the remainder of the estate, we should have thought of it before. So, this is how it happened. Dorothea bought the items from the jumble, when they got home, she asked Sybil to go up into the loft and put them in her trunk for now, which Sybil did, with all the other items of jewellery and linens etc. At some point, Dorothea went up there and muddled it all up. So, when she then gave Sybil the bag of stuff to put to one side for Mildred, worthless junk, Sybil just did as she was asked.

Not having even looked at the pearls she wouldn't have known the difference from one set or another. She kept them at the Garden centre. That was that. When Duncan asked after the stuff she told him she had it all, he then said, 'don't ever give it to charity, we will pay generously – either let us know when

Mildred has collected the items, or you've sent them down.' So, in the end you did post them down, Sybil, when Dad asked you to, simple."

"Only by this time, Walter had already taken the 'other' pearls Rosie found in the box and sold them," Sybil added.

"A few weeks after that the jewellers closed down. Rosie, you and Sybil just have to retell the story of the women at the jumble giving false names," Walter added.

"Yes, then Betsie, Sue, the hairdressers and me, can make statements about the rest of it," Rosie added.

"I just hope they all get their comeuppance, Walter, we find out what really happened and then we can put all this to bed and move forward." Jane rubbed Walter's arm reassuringly.

"Are you coming or staying, Walter? I have to get back to cook Derek's dinner."

"He's staying, Sybil. I promised him roast beef last night and it's slowly cooking," Jane winked.

"See you tomorrow then. We all know what to say. Goodbye, people!" Sybil left them alone.

"She's one very good friend you know. I'm sure she'll keep any promises she made to Dorothea and see them through to the bitter end," Rosie said.

"I just want you to know Jane, I wasn't going to keep it all; me and Rosie decided not to involve you and Anna and drag you into any trouble, once we started to find out what was going on of course."

"No explanations necessary, Walter. Now, let's go and see to this dinner. After all the fuss of last night, I thought we could spend a cosy afternoon watching old movies."

Making it official

It wasn't normal procedure to take statements anywhere else than the Police Station, as a rule. But this was Bromington-on-sea and Matthew and his constable were very laid back. Which meant, he could see the fear in Rosie's eyes on Saturday night and the way she hung her head yesterday during one interpretation by Sybil.

He wasn't here to judge family matters. What he was here for, was to gather information officially, about what could potentially turn out to be a murder. An outside team were called in that tragic weekend and over the coming days. The forensics had confirmed only one person had been the other side of the fence, most probably alone, inebriated and had slipped over the cliff edge.

According to Steven Grey, he thought his wife had gone out for the day with their friends, Jack and Sandra Hughes. When they came back alone later, on Monday, and the area of the beach was cordoned off by police, he reported his wife as possibly missing. Following the discovery of the body he was called into the local station a few hours afterwards where he formally identified Jennifer Grey. This was nothing like the movies, no cold morgue. Her husband sat at a table with the chief medical examiner present. To minimise the shock, they explained to Steven what he was about to see and then turned over the photograph of his wife, which had been lying face down. He confirmed it was her.

There had been no sign of a struggle, no marks or assault and the body was not dead until it hit the sea, she drowned. Her lungs were full of water. Jack and Sandra Hughes said they left her at the pub at 10.30. Her husband, Steven, was in there somewhere, they didn't know if they were together. When they drunk too much, they were best left alone.

The general feeling among the force was she had been arguing with her husband and she went off, drunk. The wrong way, in the dark. Maybe she'd climbed over the fence not realising it was a cliff edge. Now they realised, it probably wasn't the case at all. Worse, it may not even be Jennifer Grey, it could have been her twin sister, Janice.

Yes, on checking records they had found them. Born on the 20th September 1972. Almost forty-seven years of age, which matched the death certificate. Nee Blake. Jennifer married in July 1997 aged 24. Janice had never married. Records showed Janice lived at the same address as her sister and sister's husband up until 2010. Then there were no more records. Not just of these three, but Jack and Sandra Hughes were not on any electoral or council tax records either.

They had told police they were ex-pats, living in Spain and they came to England once or twice a year. A brief check confirmed the addresses were real, unfortunately, no further checks were deemed necessary at the time. Now the suspects were gone. They had parted company before the boat sailed.

The police were searching records of the boat. When they did trace it by its HIN number, it had been recently sold. The sellers used the same Spanish addresses which belonged to some 80-year-old residents native to their country, who lived in the sticks. They had never heard of either of the boat couples. The sellers had specifically asked for a cash transaction as the boat was jointly owned. It made for easier handling they said. The new owners had done nothing wrong, the boat now belonged to them. There was DNA evidence of five different people having previously been on the boat. Rosie was right.

Duncan Jones was in police custody. He faced several hours of police questioning and thanks to his expensive solicitor he was eventually released without charges. They had no evidence of any wrong-doing. He was free to go. He'd admitted to approaching Sybil with the view of his brother-in-law buying pearls from the Wodehouse family if they were not claimed by Mildred Wodehouse; rather than donate them to charity. It hadn't happened. He said he knew nothing about the pearls until Sybil mentioned them. Nobody could prove otherwise.

He knew nothing of his brother-in-law's whereabouts even though he had been seen in the Flag with him recently. He knew nothing of any pearls being purchased by Rumbleworth's. He certainly was not involved in anything untoward regarding customs and excise or any other matters.

There was nothing they could do, he was released. You cannot charge a person on hearsay, intuition or feelings.

The jeweller's stock had been sold lock, stock and barrel to a private consortium of investors. Matthew rightly guessed the transactions would lead to a never-ending trail and the items would be in the hands of several dealers, individuals, overseas buyers and goodness knows what. He was also convinced having found no reports anywhere in the UK of missing pearls, or insurance claims, that Walter would be in the clear and able to keep the money. Ivan had flown to Egypt, a place the British authorities had no extradition rights.

At this moment in time, the police had no inclination of where the boat people were. They could be laying low anywhere which such a large amount of money from their boat sale and paying cash everywhere they went. Matthew had a feeling they had made their way into a country via the sea and with the assistance of Duncan's contacts. After all, he wouldn't want to be implicated in anything. He was astute, he'd want them gone. His phone records were showing nothing. No contact with his brother or any one of the others. They were no longer available on the contact mobile numbers on police record.

Sandra, the hairdresser, made a statement regarding the customer's 'head' and large skin tag, explaining all. If only the body had not been cremated, they may have had good reason to dig it up and check this out. It was presumed Janice did not have this tag, but Jennifer did. It was not classed as withholding information, because Sandra hadn't been 100% sure, not until it tied in with the name her friend had called her, which didn't match the booking, but did match what the woman called herself in front of Sybil and Rosie.

The police found Mildred Wodehouse at the house of her boyfriend. She was taken to her local Police Station to make another statement, they also got her son's new address and hauled him in again too. The statements said nothing different to the originals.

If only they could find the cheap pearls, which everyone felt was totally relevant.

Tuesday morning, at long last, Rosie had some free time. All the talk over the last two days about Dorothea's treasure chest had got her thinking. She headed down to the basement quickly followed by one very small dog with an inquisitive nature.

"Don't you be charging about, Bear, there's a good boy." Of course, this fell on deaf ears as he was soon off exploring. Rosie sat cross-legged on the floor and unlocked the chest. Something she felt she would do alone. Sybil may or may not have looked in here once, sometimes or never. But Rosie respected the privacy of Dorothea while at the same time wanting to know what secrets were lurking inside.

There were all sorts inside the deep wooden chest. Family photos, lace, empty glass perfume bottles. A silver hairbrush and comb. Rosie dug deeper. Most certainly these were all personal effects. The solicitor had the official documents. Linens, pressed flowers, a music box; inside was a small key. A cold breeze swept over Rosie's arms and Bear began to bark, running around in circles.

"Shush boy, come here, come on, it's alright. I'm sure if we have a ghost, she's very friendly. Do you want me to stop, Dorothea? Make a noise if you do!" Rosie glanced upwards.

Everywhere was quiet and Rosie felt a bit silly. Bear climbed on top of her legs, peering over the top of her arms. She carried on, placing items in piles on the floor. There *were* actually some jewellery boxes. One had a beautiful watch inside. It had stopped, of course, and would probably need winding every day to keep it going. Placing it around her wrist, it fit perfectly. The cold metal soon lost its chill. Rosie later found it was a circa 1950 Omega platinum and diamond *Ladies Art Deco Cocktail Watch*. It did have monetary value, but more than that, it was stunning. Rosie wanted to keep it on, and Jane thought it was a good idea when she saw it a few days later.

Dorothea hadn't been able to find her locked diary because she had wrapped it tightly inside a frilled pillowcase. Rosie now uncovered it, together with a few hand-written letters in a beautifully bound crimson satin ribbon. Unable or unwilling to move, she sat silently for a good ten minutes waiting for any noise, any indication to put this back where she found it. There was nothing, silence rang in her ears. Rosie opened the music box, retrieving the small key. She slipped it into the diary lock, and it clicked open.

Rosie locked the chest, intending to come back tomorrow and finish sorting out the rest. She placed the pillowcase and its contents in her bottom drawer of the dressing table. Matthew was coming for dinner tonight and she wanted to cook steaks.

"Fancy a ride to the beach, Bear? I need to go to the butchers. Special dinner tonight. We can take the pushbike, Dad's put new tyres on and there's a basket for you and the shopping. Bumble, get yourself out of there; daft cat!"

Bumble hissed and protested. She was quite comfortable in the basket. Rosie had left the bike behind the sofa. "Fair enough. How about a nice walk instead then, boy?"

Bear ran over to the wall, jumping up and down and running around in circles, trying to grab his lead. He was smiling. "I take that as a yes then, even if I do have to carry you home."

The walk to the village which was usually a pleasant amble, hit a sour note today. Duncan was patrolling the far end of the harbour, holding a pad. He appeared to be inspecting the boats and writing down details. She could feel his eyes boring down on her from several metres away. Rosie couldn't shake the feeling of danger away. She hadn't been on the man's radar before, but she was now. Bear tugged on the lead, pulling her towards the soggy sand, he was digging with great gusto, kicking up golden particles, soft mud and water.

"Do you know what, boy? You've given me a great idea!"

"Hiya Rosie. Oh, look at Bear having so much fun, he's lovely. Got time for a coffee?" Izzy bent down to Bear's level, not at all bothered when he jumped up her legs, covering her jeans with all sorts of delights.

"Izzy, I'm sorry, he is a naughty boy sometimes and I can't stop him! I was just telling him; he has given me a good idea!"

"Come and tell us all about it. Look, Sandra's waving at you frantically through the salon window! Besides, Duncan is almost upon us, but don't look now."

"Come on, Bear. I'm sure our friends have a treat for you." Everywhere they went, someone had something to give the adorable puppy.

A gruff voice called out behind them. "Are you going to come back and clear your dog's mess up? Can't you read? A one thousand pound fine for fouling on this beach."

"Excuse me?" Rosie fumed. "I always clear up after my pet and I resent that remark."

"Oh, you do, do you, what's this then?" Duncan screwed his eyes tightly and a sneer formed on his top lip. He was pointing to something which had obviously been there for some time and was far too big to have belonged to Bear.

"Clear it up and we'll say no more about it, or do you want me to take photographic evidence?"

The man was deliberately being confrontational, and Rosie wasn't going to give him the satisfaction of trying to intimidate her. "Fine," she said, scooping the offensive pile into a bag and placing it in the dog bin. The only mess the pup had made was a hole in the sand and now, sneakily cocking his leg up, watering Duncan's shoe.

"Come on, Bear, let's go," Rosie chirped. "Good boy." Izzy was trying not to laugh at the pup's antics, which only the women had seen.

"What a dick!" Izzy fumed, once they were back inside the salon.

"Blimey, no customers?" Rosie walked towards one of the sinks. "Can I wash my hands?"

"Of course. We just wondered if you'd heard anything more?"

"No, Sandra." Rosie explained it all up to date. "I've had an idea, well two actually. I think it all depends on finding these pearls. Me and Dad have been to all the local jewellers, no luck. When Bear was playing, it got me to thinking. What if Janice, or Jennifer had them when she fell? Someone stole my mother's pearls. Nobody goes to the small beachy area directly underneath the cliffs because if the tide comes in you will get trapped. Plus, you can only get there by boat."

"What does this have to do with Bear digging? You can't take him there to dig!"

"No, not him, but what about a specially trained police dog? A long shot I know, but I do still have a cardigan of my mother's she left it in Dad's car and he gave it to me, in case she showed up here, he didn't want to see her and I never did, so..."

"If a dog picks up the scent there could be an outside chance if the pearls were on the rocks or buried just under the sand..." Izzy replied.

"The dog might find them, and there'd be an outside chance of getting some fingerprints?" Sandra said, enthusiastically.

"Yes. Exactly that. The police concentrated on the cliff edge, then the body was swept around with the tide and washed up on the harbour beach," Rosie explained.

"So, the coved area where nobody goes could have been overlooked, because it's only recently come to light about the pearls."

"Yes, Izzy. Worth a shot, don't you think?"

"Totally, Rosie. They can probably still pick up fingerprints or DNA or something and guess what we've been doing. Go on, Sandra tell her, it was your idea!"

"Well, because I felt guilty for not coming forward sooner, I've made up for it. Look!" Opening a drawer, Sandra pulled out several labelled plastic bags. "Cool huh! I've been taking hair samples from all the customers, because, well, just because. And because we're unisex it means the men too."

"Including Duncan?"

"Yes, Rosie. I took great pleasure pulling one of his hairs out," Sandra laughed.

"She had me at it too, so we have quite a collection. Well, you never know, do you?"

"Clever ladies. Aren't they clever, Bear!"

Izzy took out a plastic box, full of small bone treats and gave one to Bear. "Not that easy, pal. Give me your paw, good boy!"

"I don't think he knows how; he is too naughty!" Rosie laughed.

"Is that so? This pup has you wrapped around his little finger. Show your mummy what you can do, Bear. Give me your paw."

With gentle encouragement with her hand behind his leg, Bear lifted his paw and got his treat. He tried it on one more time. He sat again, tail wagging.

"Paw, Bear." He lifted his paw and got himself another treat.

"Good boy. See, Rosie, he's not that naughty."

"Thanks for the coffee ladies, I have to rush. Matthew is coming for tea and I'm pulling out all the stops!"

"Oh, he is, is he?" Sandra smiled. "Well don't make anything with garlic then."

"I was thinking steak, new potatoes and salad. What do you reckon?"

"Pull out all the stops, Rosie. And then tell him about your idea and don't forget to let him know about our samples, we've gone to a lot of hard work you know," Izzy smiled.

"Well, I hope he likes cheesecake too. I have beer and wine and a friendly demeanour. Besides, I want to be an investigator, it's fun isn't it?"

"The coast is clear at least. Duncan has got in his car and driven off."

"Probably discovered his wet sock and trouser leg," Rosie smirked.

An unexpected retrieval

They had only met three times. The first was a little blurry and sped far too quickly. Next, it was a brief encounter in a room full of people. Rosie's stomach was flipping over, wow. Glancing at the clock she fussed around the table once more. Straightening the cutlery, re-wiping the glasses, trying to fold the serviettes into something clever.

"Ouch, Bumble. Jeez, don't do that!" Rosie rubbed the back of her leg where her cat had dug her claws in. "Damn, look, you've made a hole in my tights. Shoo, cat, go on, chase some birds or something!" The buzzer rang. "Oh, no. He's early. Bumble you better scarper; go, go and play."

Rosie rushed past the mirror, rubbed the lipstick from the side of her mouth, only to remember she had cream on her finger, serves her right for being greedy, licking from the bowl. The buzzer rang again, and she pressed the intercom. "Come in, Matthew."

She opened the door in her laddered tights and smudged face. "I'm sorry," she spluttered.

"For what?" he laughed. Before he could pass over the lovely bunch of flowers, Bear came charging in the room barking and showing off two big muddy paws and a dirty nose.

"Oh no, I took my eyes off him, look out!"

"Look, Bear. I have something for you too!"

The little dog stopped in his tracks and began sniffing the yummy scrummy doggy treat in the shape of a big bone, which he made a grab for and ran away. Straight out through the cat-flap.

There, sitting in the middle of the dining table, was an arrogant Bumble. She'd decided now was the perfect time to wash her private regions and clean her ears.

Rosie breathed in sharply and let out a long sigh. Could anything else possibly go wrong in such a short space of time. Matthew put his arms on her shoulders and gave her a cheeky kiss on the back of the neck.

"Let me tell you something. I have two dogs who dominate the lounge. You can't sit down without accumulating legs full of dog's hairs. And I have a cat who I'm convinced is the devil incarnate. Or words to that effect. He's black with red eyes I'm sure; he catches birds in flight and makes Bumble look like Mother Teresa."

Matthew felt Rosie laughing before he heard her. "The table looks lovely, but how about we play the pets at their own game? Leave them to the kitchen and when the food's ready we can eat on trays in the lounge. I really don't mind."

Rosie was laughing so much she snorted. Devil incarnate, Mother Teresa. There, *now* it couldn't get any worse. Matthew burst out laughing too. They were going to have a great night.

"Anyway, call me Matt. Only my parents call me Matthew."

"I'm sure you told me that on Saturday. I forgot."

Not being the centre of attention anymore, Bumble strode along the table-top, over every work surface she could and then jumped from the window-ledge.

"Do you want me to close it?"

"Please, I'll put the potatoes on," Rosie answered. At least if Bear came running back in, he couldn't get on the table. Matt wasted no time running a clean cloth over the surfaces, opened the fridge and made himself useful. He took the salad out and passed the raw steaks over.

"These look lovely, fresh from the butcher's! Wine, Rosie?"

"Please. I got beer too."

"I'll only have the one, I'm driving."

"Whoa look at this! I hope I didn't spoil your surprise. How did you know cheesecake is my favourite dessert?"

"I didn't. It's mine, so...!"

Matt set the table with sauces and even found a vase for the flowers.

"They are lovely, thank you. I didn't get a chance to say that."

"Because you were too busy trying to impress me. I think your cat did a good job on your leg!"

Maybe an hour ago, Rosie Wodehouse would have cringed at the ladders running up her leg. Not anymore.

"Cheers Matt. Tuck in; with a bit of luck they should be medium-rare."

The enticing smell soon had the young pup racing through from the garden again, he was getting a bit plump for the cat-flap.

"No chance, pal!" Matt laughed.

Neither of them felt shy eating in front of each other, several times they held their gazes and more than once they shared a good laugh. This was perfect, nothing too heavy on their minds... for now.

Together they cleared the kitchen. "That was the best cheesecake I've ever had. Seriously. You're hired. No, I'm joking. Next time come to me. I promise you the best baked beans on the planet."

"What, no toast?"

"Don't they class that as multi-tasking?"

"Silly. I hope you don't mind me mixing business with pleasure, Matt - but I've had an idea. Two in fact. Say no if you want to, and I'm not quite sure how much of it is legal or anything, but that part wasn't down to me!"

"Sounds intriguing. Tell me all about it." The two of them settled down on the sofa. Predictably, Bear kept trying to jump up between them. Matt lifted him and he climbed onto Matt's legs where he sat upright, listening in on the conversation.

"If I'm honest," Matt said, after he'd heard Rosie out, "I'm not sure if the force will fund any more investigating in the area, due to cutbacks, but I hear what you're saying. When I said I have two dogs, I didn't mention they are trained police dogs. The thing is, you can't get around to that area unless you go by boat and then it has to be at low tide. It isn't beach so much as rocks, but there is a small inlet."

"Like a cave you mean?"

"A small one, yes."

"So, if we went there with your dogs on a low tide, secured the boat then we could have a good look around the area and the inlet."

"We? No, Rosie, it's far too dangerous in that area and if the tide came in early you would be trapped."

"I'm an excellent swimmer. We can use life jackets for us and the dogs. Oh, please, Matt. Say you'll think about it at least. I can't settle until this is all over, if it weren't for these blasted pearls none of this would have happened."

"None of it was your fault, or your dad's. Seems they smuggled them in, you got caught up in it all and then they thought they could take them back, but it ended in tragedy. I do understand how you feel though. We were instructed by forensics it was an open and shut case. If not for you, they would have got away with it."

"Whoever did it still will, if we can't find the pearls, and potentially a murderer."

"Do you have your mother's cardigan? Let me take it with me and give it some thought."

"The hairdresser's have done well too, haven't they!"

"They have, if they managed to get the hair follicles, we can't get DNA without it. Remember, we might not be able to pinpoint anyone if we find the box of pearls, but we can at least eliminate anyone who doesn't have fingerprints or DNA in or on the box. That's if it hasn't been submerged in water. We only have a good chance of lifting anything in the first six weeks."

"Okay, Matt. Worth a try though isn't it? Coffee?"

"Love one, but don't ask me to watch a chick's flick. I draw the line at retaining some of my macho exterior!"

By eleven o'clock after a lingering goodnight kiss and cuddle, Matt left. Rosie couldn't remember the last time she'd had such a nice evening and her new man was a real gent. Because he'd invited her out on Friday for a meal, she felt like they were an item.

The streaming sunlight peaked through a gap in the curtains. Rosie had spent the evening before stargazing before finally nodding off. Was it eight o'clock already? It was late for her. Bear was snuggled on the pillow next to her and when she stretched out, Rosie discovered Bumble at the bottom of the bed. What was this, a sleepover!?

"Good morning animals. I hope you slept well. Come on Bear, off to the garden." Rosie wanted a shower in peace, a light breakfast and then she had plans for a quiet morning with Dorothea's diary. Bumble would soon run off when she heard the power shower.

Rosie had refused Jane and Anna's offer of going into town today when they finished at the B & B – she needed to have some down time to catch up with a few things. Besides, it hadn't gone unnoticed that Walter popped round three or four times a week now; he went straight up to see Jane and being on the bottom floor, Rosie couldn't help but also recognise the sound of Brandon's shoes. He had a habit of running down the last few stairs before he ever left the building.

Taking a deep breath, Rosie decided to start with the diary. Bear had settled back down for his morning sleep and the ladies had gone off to town. They would all catch up for a good gossip on Friday lunchtime. She had the grace to wait ten minutes, to make sure nothing fell off a shelf or anything like that. However, she was sure someone was in the kitchen with her.

"Here goes then, Dorothea. I'm reading your private stuff." Nursing a warm cup of coffee, Rosie began. The diary didn't begin until Dorothea was in her mid-twenties. 1950 to be precise, Dorothea was twenty-seven years old. Five years older than her brother, William, who had just turned twenty-two. Dorothea affectionately referred to him as Billy.

It seemed Dorothea had a sweetheart back then, but he hadn't returned home from the war. Missing in action. According to the diary he was just eighteen when war broke out and was conscripted within a year. Dorothea was seventeen years old and he'd been her only sweetheart. Something she kept a secret by all accounts. Her boyfriend, Charles, was just nineteen when she last saw him.

When Billy was twenty-eight, after having two or three girlfriends, he met Nana. Sylvia Wodehouse. The year was 1956. Dorothea shunned any attention paid towards her. Her heart belonged to Charles, her secret love. It seems her parents would never have approved. Not only because she was too young, but his family came from a very poor background, they only wanted the best for their daughter.

While Billy spent his time with his father at the gardening business, Dorothea was happy to stay here, in the house, helping her mother with the Bed & Breakfast business. They were a very wealthy family, money handed down through the generations. The silver spoons Miss. D. Wodehouse called herself and hers.

There was something about Sylvia which Dorothea could not take to. She saw no love in the woman's eyes, just greed. Billy was too daft to spot it for himself. He worked hard six days a week building up the business while his girlfriend did very little.

Eventually, after a year or so, Dorothea took it upon herself to keep a closer watch on Sylvia, who was now Billy's fiancée. They had set a date for their wedding in six months from now.

As Miss Wodehouse now had her own car and plenty of spare hours to herself she began to follow her.

The first time she found her in the company of a man, it was in broad daylight, they were walking around in Bromington Town. There was nothing untoward as such, but alas, Dorothea lost sight of them in the busy market. On one or two other occasions she spotted her around and about with gentleman friends. She casually dropped it in conversation with Billy, but it went over his head. When Sylvia got to hear about it, she persuaded Billy after they got wed, to move away with her, away from his meddling sister. Their parents gave Billy a large sum of money for a substantial deposit on the bungalow Walter had been born in, in 1959.

The majority of Dorothea's diary centred on her brother. She loved him dearly and did not want to see him get hurt. He lived too far away, but Dorothea got it in her mind to hire someone and soon found out Sylvia was still out and about, up to no good. She made a note of the days and the times, there was a pattern to it all.

Dorothea booked herself a few days away, to be near her brother. She went to his workplace and told him what was going on, just as she'd tried to in the past. She insisted if he went to a certain hotel that day, he would find out himself. He agreed, but informed his sister if it wasn't true, he didn't want to see her anymore. Sylvia had sworn months ago Dorothea was trying to wreck their marriage for no good reason.

Only William never made it that day. In his haste, he drove recklessly. His car came off the road and the accident, was fatal.

Dorothea had never forgiven herself, torturing her mind. If it wasn't for her, then her brother would still be alive. It was true, Sylvia had admitted to many affairs over the years, she never cared for William Wodehouse, she'd only married him for his money. And what was more, she told Dorothea if her parents did not help her and Walter, she would deny everything and they would forever more blame Dorothea for the loss of their only son, believing Sylvia to be innocent of any wrongdoing.

And so it was. Sylvia got her lump sum and her mortgage was paid off. After the funeral she never saw the family again and Dorothea never uttered another word to her. Rosie found it hard to see, her watery eyes blurring her vision. It was true what they said, money didn't buy happiness, what was left over was passed down to Walter, he added to it and recently passed it down to Rosie. Now she knew the truth behind it, it made her very sad. Not only had Dorothea lost her only love, she had lost her brother too and spent the rest of her life alone; apart from her pets.

Her coffee was stone cold. Rosie put the kettle on for a cup of tea instead, peaked at Bear who was snoring, and then she blew her nose and wiped her eyes. The diary really had got to her. She must not ever, ever share this with anyone. It would break her dad's heart. His mother, his wife, were both love cheats and users, Michael had used him all his life. It seemed only Rosie deeply cared for him, and Jane did of course, they were having fun.

Now, after all this time, Rosie knew something her dad had never known. Did Sybil know? There was no way of knowing if she had gone through Dorothea's private stuff or not. Then the diary went on and so forth. Eventually, Dorothea was the sole heir of everything and in turn, Sybil and Derek were bequeathed a house and a sum of money. Dorothea made it her business to keep a distant watch on Walter. Her guilt consumed her, she blamed herself for the boy being fatherless.

When history repeated itself years down the line with Mildred it consumed Dorothea once more. She would never leave the woman anything. Of course, she could have chosen to leave everything she had to Sybil and Derek, or directly to charity. She didn't want to do that.

There was nothing she didn't know. Like Rosie, she had an enquiring mind. Dorothea was well-aware of Michael's father, who he was and where he lived. Everything was written down, this was all new information for Rosie to digest now, since Michael had altered his Facebook to private. Michael's father was a swindler and had built a business on deceit. Well, this was news, it had been Michael's intention for a good few years to trace his father and emigrate apparently. He too, would not benefit from the will, not in any shape or form.

Dorothea knew Walter worked hard all his life, it was only once his mother died, was the will changed. For Sylvia was another who would never benefit. It choked Rosie up when she started reading about herself.

That poor child has never been given anything. She has led a downtrodden life, unlike her half- brother. Still, she has made a go and got on as best she can, never asking for anything. There is only one person in this world who I would like to benefit from my monetary good fortune and that is Rosalyn Wodehouse. My hope is that she turns this big empty house into a loving home, and she will carry on with the business my mother and myself built up. If I'd ever had children, I would have been more than happy for a daughter just like her.

Rosie was now blubbing away, tears streaming down her face, salty and warm. This time, Bear woke up and plodded over to her. "Come here, boy; give Mummy a big cuddle," she blurted. It was time for lunch, and she made herself a big, comforting, cheese and pickle sandwich and a bowl of biscuits and meat for Bear. "Let's open the bottom half of the door. You're getting too round for the flap." A warm breeze swept in and Rosie could smell the lovely clean laundry she'd hung out earlier.

"Maybe this afternoon we can play in the garden. I have a bit more reading first baby Bear."

The pup wasn't listening, he'd found his plastic flowerpots which he spent hours chasing around with.

The diary then turned to Walter. Of course, there is one more person I want to see have everything he so rightly deserves. But not that blasted wife of his; I hope he sees sense eventually! Dorothea's hope for Walter was to meet a nice lady, move to Bromington and spend his days at the lovely Riverside Cottage.

"I don't know if you can hear me, Great Aunt Dorothea, but it is all falling into place. If only you could give me a sign about the whereabouts of the pearls! Your prank has rather opened up a can of worms!"

And here it was, the trip to the Village Hall and the fun she'd had with Sybil buying some cheap items to gift to the detestable Mildred. After that, there was only one more entry, it did say Dorothea kept forgetting where her diary had got to, her memory wasn't what it used to be, and then it finished. Rosie locked it up and put the key in her pocket. All there was left to read now were the letters.

On opening the first one she could see they were from Charles, Dorothea's lost sweetheart. All of them. Secret letters, from her secret man.

This *certainly* wasn't any of her business. Rosie tied the letters back together and took everything to the basement, placing it into the chest. Maybe tomorrow she would empty it properly and find a home for everything.

Just as she came back upstairs the front door opened.

"Rosie boo-boo! Here you are, a minute on the lips and all that. Sorry, darling, couldn't resist. Must rush, kiss, kiss!" Anna took the stairs two at a time, leaving her friend with a wonderful white and blue gingham checked box. A delicious fresh cream pastry of gigantic proportions stared up at her.

"Thank you, friend. When will I ever start this diet?"

"Nonsense!" Jane tapped her on the bottom. "There's nothing of you. Are we meeting Friday?"

"Yes, pile round as always!"

"Great Rosie, must dash darling!" Jane planted a soppy kiss on her cheek and rushed upstairs too.

The following day, Rosie got her gardening gloves on bright and early. She'd promised her furry friends a morning in the garden. Dad had left a few plants outside her door last night which would go lovely in the rockery. He didn't even knock.

Meanwhile, just after lunch, Matthew and two of his men had just returned from the inlet area directly under the cliff. There was no way he would have allowed Rosie out there with such a strong undercurrent. It had been well worth the journey. At the very back of the small cave the water didn't always reach, and a box had been dragged in by the tide and was tightly wedged between two rocks. It was now bagged up as potential evidence.

The missing pearls

The good news was, Matthew was fairly sure the box had been dragged inside the cave with the first incoming tide on the night of the accident. Meaning, there was every chance they had stayed just out of reach and out of low tidal waters over the last few weeks. The tides had not been too high according to the charts. The body, being much heavier, had gone in and out and been carried around the coastline.

Following recent new evidence, the case was now officially re-opened and being treated as suspicious. For now, Matthew was keeping the news to himself, with the hope within twenty-four hours he would have some positive news.

Meanwhile, he was tracing anyone local for fingerprint records and he was going to arrange for Mildred Wodehouse and her son to provide fingerprints at their local station so they could eliminate anyone who had valid reason to have touched the pearls.

It was a long shot, but Matthew had a team going back for any records of Jack and Sandra Hughes, Steven Grey, Jennifer Grey nee Blake and Janice Blake.

"You've found my pearls? Where were they, who stole them? I jolly well hope you have arrested the culprit. And why do you need my fingerprints exactly?" Mildred shrieked.

"We have already explained all of this, Madam. Please take a seat, the duty officer will be with you in a minute."

"Has my son turned up yet?"

"What is his name?" The desk sergeant asked.

"Michael. Michael Smith. Don't be impertinent young man. It was you who requested we attend. In any case, it will be pointless fingerprinting him, he never touched the pearls or the case. Waste of police time and public money."

"We've got a right old battleaxe in reception, Jerry. Can we hurry her along?" Constable Bradley Stimpson asked his Sergeant.

"What, and spoil my fun! Now our new man out there knows what the job feels like. My missus could give her a run for her money. No, let him stew, make her wait for a while!"

And they did. For a whole hour. Eventually, Mildred Wodehouse was called into a small room where her fingerprints were taken.

Michael still hadn't arrived when she left and she wasn't staying a moment longer. She'd never been so humiliated in all her life and the blue ink was still on her fingers.

Arthur Green sincerely regretted the day he clapped eyes on her. Now he was getting it in the neck every day, the same as poor Walter had done for years on end. It was a relief to finally be sleeping in a separate bedroom. The time was approaching when he would kick her out. She wasn't his problem. A bloodsucker, that's what she was. Only another couple of weeks to go and then Mildred's divorce was final, and she couldn't go after Walter for anything. Arthur could wait that long. He owed the old boy that much. She could go and live with her son.

Friday morning and the results were due back by lunchtime. Rosie still had no idea what was going on. Walter had been to the station as requested as had the local villagers, including

Duncan Jones. Although Matthew was convinced, he wasn't involved in this potential murder. He was determined to see him eventually face charges for aiding and abetting smugglers. Handling stolen goods. The man knew a lot, possibly including the whereabout of the boat people. Perhaps if murder could be proven he would be a little more forthcoming.

Matthew had no luck tracing any records of the boat people. But the good news was, the fingerprint examiners had some results for them.

The people known to have handled the pearls had been identified. There were just two sets of prints unknown. One set on the box and the pearls. The other just on the box.

They were still waiting for one person to provide their prints. Michael Smith, who was unavailable. A call was put out to go to his address and trace his whereabouts, urgently.

Right at this moment in time, Michael Smith was halfway across the world on a flight to Australia. Should he have willingly given his prints, no doubt he would have come up with a believable story. Maybe taking his mother to her room, removing the pearls as she was making herself noticed. Any excuse which would give him a reason to have touched the box.

Instead he panicked, he ran.

For indeed, on the night of the tragedy, he did take his mother to her room, but not before dropping a tablet into her drink earlier. He then removed the pearls from her bag because according to Janice Blake they were worth a fortune. Yes, she had been there all the time. Only one woman was ever seen. The twins worked well together, providing alibis, keeping each other out of trouble while working as the main scammers abroad. This time they had stuck around for far too long, waiting for the pearls to come to light. The pearls that Duncan had talked them into leaving in the jumble. He was due to get a fair cut, like he always did.

So, it wasn't Jennifer Grey in the Flag that night, she went out last time. No, it was Janice Blake, fooling everyone they were one and the same. Michael followed the woman out to the toilets, he convinced her to get him a large sum of money and he told her he would get the pearls and meet her behind the church.

The only people Mildred had heard screaming were revellers below her room, she was in no fit state to know where she was.

The boat people knew the pearls were worth several hundreds of thousands. The fact this fool only wanted ten thousand was fine by Jack and Sandra, who supplied the money. They intended to cut Duncan out and take them elsewhere. They could have lost a lot of money because of his mistake. Jack thought he could get at least eight hundred thousand for them and that is where they were going the next day, to look for another buyer. Neither of them knew Janice hadn't returned until the morning. All of them believed she had double-crossed them. True to form, Steven had been well and truly drunk, not even aware his wife, Jennifer, was sleeping beside him all night. She did go out with Jack and Sandra the following day, while he was asleep. When they returned and saw the police, Jennifer left the area.

When he identified his wife as dead, he really did think it was her at the time. She wasn't around. Jack and Sandra told him Janice was out and he didn't know anything about the evening before. The Hughes' and Jennifer had hatched a plan, and for that, Steven needed to believe his wife was dead.

So, Jack and Sandra had gone back to their boat at 10.30 as they said. They made sure they were seen. They took the money from the safe and gave it to Janice. Michael went to the

Lobster Pot after he walked Betsie home. Five minutes after checking into his room he snuck out. With a gun. It wasn't real, but it looked real enough.

Janice took the path behind the pub, making sure no-one saw her as she crept along being as quiet as she could. After several glasses of wine, she was a little unsteady on her feet. Michael walked up the steep hill and made sure he went no further than the church door, he waited in the dark.

A while later a voice called out to him. "I'm here, where are you?"

"Over here," he called. "Do you have the money?"

"Do you have the pearls?"

They both said they did. As a gesture of goodwill, Michael gave her the box and let her look inside as well, she picked the pearls up and she couldn't tell the difference between those and the real ones. She put them back and held the box tightly.

"Money." Michael said.

She gave it to him. Ten bundles. He had no clear idea if each one contained a thousand, but it looked close enough.

"Go and stand over there, don't leave here for ten minutes. I don't want to be seen with you."

Janice began walking over towards the cliff edge and then the fireworks began. Lighting up the sky. Michael had no need to show the replica gun and hurried off back towards the Lobster Pot. He'd already worked out his mother would be in no fit state early tomorrow and he was going to insist they leave early. With a bit of luck, she'd have no idea her precious pearls were gone.

In Janice's drunken state she had climbed over the small fence because she needed the toilet. Of course, she had no idea how close she was to the edge until it was too late. Her screams were drowned out with the noise of the fireworks and the revellers. So, in fact, there had been no murder. It was a tragic accident.

And now Michael Smith was making himself look as guilty as sin. In a moment of blind panic, he had fled. All along he wanted to wait a few weeks to leave or he would have raised suspicion with his mother. When he did go, he wanted her to believe he'd had regular contact with his father who had paid for his flight.

Michael Smith was eventually picked up when his plane touched down at Adelaide airport and he was held in custody on suspicion of murder. His statement proved otherwise.

He never did get to meet his father and spent several months on remand back in the UK before he went to court and told his story. He was not found guilty of murder or manslaughter. He still faced lesser charges of failing to give fingerprints, carrying a firearm - as nobody knew if it was real or not, he had disposed of it, theft, assaulting a police officer which he did on his arrest, assault on the second degree for administering drugs. All of it together was enough to give him a five-year prison sentence.

The judge did award damages to Mildred Wodehouse. In the sum of £10,000. To be paid to the court by Michael Smith. There was never a mention of another set of very valuable pearls. Neither did Matthew disclose the fact one set of prints belonged to a young man who worked at a jewellers in Bromington. The very place Walter had purchased the cheap pearls.

One year later

It could only have been presumed at some point, Jennifer Grey had come out of hiding and the Hughes would have told Steven Grey his wife was in fact, alive, and Janice was dead. They were all leaving by separate ways and if the police thought Jennifer Grey was deceased and knew nothing of Janice, she could at least not have to look over her shoulder, she was officially deceased! Or so she thought, she now travelled as Janice Blake using her deceased sister's I.D.

There was never any claim anywhere in countries connected to the UK via Interpol about any large insurance claim for pearls. Two months after matters died down in Bromington, Duncan had left. The boat people were never found. Rosie believed they had all regrouped somewhere around the world, no doubt scamming and smuggling all over again. New boat, maybe new identities. All they had left behind were very probably Janice Blake's ashes.

"Who knows," Rosie said to her dad one evening. Maybe when Michael gets out, his father will take him in?"

"Do you know what, dear? I couldn't care less. Your mother ended up being housed by the council, a small flat somewhere and she got more than she deserved in the end."

"She's not my mother, nor your wife. As far as I'm concerned both her and Michael Smith can rot."

"I'll drink to that, Rosie!"

"It was good news all around in the end and now you've done plenty of things for the community, with the money from the pearls; I think you can settle down with whatever funds you have left, Dad."

"There wasn't too much left from the £500,000. Pocket change. I'm okay, I still had some left over after I gave you the family money, plus a bit of change after I bought my new car from the bungalow share. Bromington-on-sea has done very well.

A new, church roof. High safety fencing all along our part of the coast. New flooring in the Village Hall, not to mention a brand-new kitchen. CCTV along the harbour and some new equipment for the youth club. Plus, a generous token bequest in Dorothea's will in Judith's favour. In the end, it was money well spent. As far as anyone knows, it was *all* donated by Dorothea."

"Well she has done an awful lot for the community! In a roundabout way; the bench dedicated to her on the quayside is a great place to sit and watch the sea. And who knows? Maybe she had a hand in it all somehow, in the end."

"I have everything I want, Rosie, but there is one thing I need."

"What's that, Dad?"

"A bit of help with choosing the very best bridesmaid's dresses for you and Anna."

"What!" Rosie jumped up, hugging her dad tightly. "Really?"

"Yes. Really. And of course, I hope you'll both help my beautiful bride to be in choosing her dress."

"Try and stop us. Oh, Dad, that's wonderful news. I don't know what to say. Jane is going to make a wonderful wife."

"There's just one thing. That's if you don't mind, of course."

"What's that?"

"I would very much like my new bride to come and live with me, if it's okay with you."

"Don't be daft, of course. The cottage is beautiful."

"Yes, and I thought she could help out in the café with Sybil as her sister is retiring. Would you mind very much getting someone else in to help with the cooking and the running of this place?"

"Leave it with me. Betty has done so well over the last year or so, she deserves to put her feet up. Maybe I can find someone suitable to live in on the middle floor. I've learnt so much with Matt's help and I really do want to keep doing my investigating you know!"

"Well, let's hope we don't have a real murder around here then. Luckily the other incident was a false alarm."

"I hope not too! Something a bit less harsh."

"Talking of which, when are you and your fiancé going to tie the knot?"

"There's no rush, Dad. After all, we aren't as old as you!"

"Cheeky so and so. Does Anna still see her young man?"

"Oh, now and then. But we still manage to catch up once a week. Hey, Dad, I hope she doesn't leave too. I don't want to be left alone in this rambling big house, just like Dorothea."

"I wonder why she never married?"

"Perhaps she never found the right man. We'll never know, will we?"

"I don't suppose we will. Just the same as I won't ever find out why she disliked my mother so much."

"Perhaps some things are better left not knowing, Dad.

"Where's that little Bear? I haven't seen him for a while."

"He isn't so little anymore. Probably asleep on my bed, he can jump up now!"

"Well. I will leave him be then. You can let Jane know you know our little secret now, she wanted me to tell you first."

"When's the big day?"

"August. The end of August almost. Saturday the 24th."

"What? Oh, my goodness. We need to get our skates on. Where's the reception?"

"The Village Hall of course. Jane told me to leave everything with you ladies. I haven't got a clue. Maybe you can help me with a suit and everything. I want your Matt to be my best man, if that's alright with you two."

"He'll be delighted. The answer's yes."

"Well. I'll be off then. I have work to do at the Garden Centre."

"Goodbye, Dad. Let's catch up at the weekend, make some plans."

"You bet," he called as he left.

Rosie felt tearful and suddenly alone. What if Anna did leave? She might move in with her boyfriend. And then her and Matt could split up, anything was possible. Was she destined to be another Dorothea? Oh my god, what if Matthew was killed doing his duty, just like Charles.

Now Rosie was having palpitations and struggling to breathe. She was starting to have a panic attack, her face felt warm and her palms sweated. What if the Wodehouse home was cursed?

Suddenly a crash in the other room made her jump. "What was that?" She tip-toed along, afraid of what she might see.

No, it wasn't possible. There on the floor, in the middle of the kitchen was the air vent built into the outside wall, it had fallen out. But how? On top of it was a large brown envelope. What? Now on top of her panic attack, Rosie was freaking out good and proper. Snatching the envelope with trembling hands she threw it on the table and opened the fridge. A cool glass of Pinot Grigio would calm her down. She took several large gulps and inhaled deeply.

Now it made sense. Bear poked his head into the gap. How on earth had he managed to push that heavy thing inwards with his small body? Perhaps it didn't make sense. He was covered in cobwebs and dust. "Go back out, Bear, go on, before you get stuck."

Rosie picked the vent up and pushed him backwards, then she put some heavy pans down in front of it, until she could get it repaired.

What could possibly have been hidden in the wall and then pushed out by a small dog, just as she was about to be totally hysterical?

"Is this you, Dorothea? Cos I'm starting to freak out now." Now she knew it was not her imagination. The kettle just switched itself on. "Does this mean I should, or I should not read this?"

Bumble jumped on the windowsill to come in, her hair shot up and she ran back out. Even Bear stood with his head in the cat flap, not wanting to come any closer.

"Wine's fine, if you don't mind, Dorothea. Let me see this then." Rosie gingerly pulled open the stuck end of the envelope. The buzzer went and she jumped out of her skin. Her pounding heart was banging in her ears.

"Sorry, Boo-boo, I forgot my key. Hey what's up? You look like you've seen a ghost."

"Well, there's one in here, that's for sure. Just tell me something, are you planning on leaving, anytime, soon?"

"Not for the next million years. Give me one of those glasses, you are freaking me out now. What's going on?"

Anna pulled a chair up and put her arm around Rosie's shoulder.

"Well, Dad said he's getting married. Did you know?"

"Not till last night, but I was sworn to secrecy until he told you; isn't it wonderful!"

"Well, yes, of course. But then Dad said Jane was moving out, which of course, she would. Then I thought, what if Anna went too and left me here, and then if Matt left, I would be just like Dorothea, a lonely old spinster!"

"Have another drink!"

"Thank you. So, you aren't going anytime soon then, with Brandon or anything?"

"Rosie boo-boo. Have you seen where Brandon lives? Right on top of a noisy street, full of pollution. Hell no! Besides, I'm not the marrying kind. Not yet, anyway. But what if you... well, you might get married and then have children, then understandably, you will want the whole house, and Mum will be gone, and I would be a gooseberry with nowhere to go!"

"Can we make a pact, right here, right now, Anna Rose! I will never chuck you out, and you will never leave! If you got married or even had children, we've both got plenty of room we could all stay right here! And if I didn't have children and you did, then ask me to be a Godparent. Then if anything happened to me, I'd pass the house down to you."

"Deal. Now where's this ghost?"

"Well, that's the thing. I had a big panic and then a crash came from in here. The grate was on the floor and this big brown envelope. It was hidden in the wall. Bear put his head through, but he can't have pushed that out, could he?"

"And you think it's the spirit of Dorothea?"

"Well as soon as I poured wine, the kettle switched itself on."

"I've seen her."

"You what?" Rosie's wine dribbled down her chin.

"A few times. She isn't scary and mainly she stays upstairs with me."

"Are you nuts, Anna. Really?"

"Mum has seen her lots too. I think I've got her sensitivity."

"Does she speak with you?"

"No, she looks out of the window, or over my shoulder when I'm painting. But if I have company, well, you know, she duly disappears."

"I'm going to open this envelope."

"Go on then. I'm dying to see."

"What if... what if it's something personal, you know, to Dorothea?"

"Well, you look first then and don't show me until you're sure it isn't."

Her hands weren't shaking anymore, and Rosie pulled out a wedge of papers.

'Suitable families to live inside Wodehouse – and those not'

In order of suitability:

Wodehouse: Rosalyn, Walter and Jane (nee Rose)

Walker: Matthew and Rosalyn (nee Wodehouse) and children

Stimpson: Bradley and Anna (nee Rose) and children

Unsuitable:

Taylor: Brandon

"Whoa, whoa, stop. Rosie. Hold on, this is crazy! Don't tell me if there's anymore. How the heck can this have been written, whenever? Years in the past and come to light now? Do you know what this means? Apart from the fact I will break up with Brandon Taylor sometime in the future! Dorothea could see into the future. This is... nuts!"

"Here; have some more wine. Well, for a start, it's telling us we are both going to be married, have children and stay in the house, the pact we only just made! But it's also saying Dad and Jane will live here. What does that mean? What's going to happen to the Garden Centre?"

"Maybe it just means we shouldn't let anyone else live here? Or I mean, you shouldn't, it's your house."

"No. No it isn't, Anna. Don't you see. It's our house."

"At least you have the right man already. I've been with Brandon on and off for a year."

"On and off, Anna. On and off. You are moving onto something better."

"What's the rest of it all about?"

"I'm a bit scared to look. Argh! No way. Look at this. Wodehouse Mystery Agency."

"Let me see that! Rosie; it's telling you about the near future and your first real case as an investigator. Look, you are licensed and everything."

"What Dorothea is telling us, Anna, is we belong here, together, and we have our destinies mapped out before us, we don't have to be afraid. I don't have to be afraid."

"Does it say when I'm going to meet my proper man, was there anyone else before him? Maybe just give me a clue, go on!"

"No. I'm going to lock this away in the chest and never look at it again. Well, maybe in a year's time we can have a peek. See how far we've come."

"You better start making a move to get this license of yours, Rosie boo-boo."

"And you are in charge of the hiring and firing, we need more staff."

"I'm on it, but there's one job we are doing together."

"What's that?"

"Sorting out this wedding of course. We can't leave them to their own devices. Can't have Mum turning up like Sandie Shaw bare-footed and floppy hatted."

"Was it her, or was it Petula Clark or someone?"

"I'm not sure, but you get my drift."

"Yes. And I don't think it's a good idea for Izzy to do her hair."

"That's a definite no."

"Are we allowed to pick our own bridesmaid dresses?"

"I think we should, Boo-boo."

"Before you protest, I'm buying our bridesmaid dresses, or at least the material. How about a dusky pink covered in antique lace - 20's style, Anna?"

"You know whatever it is, Mum will probably end up making them and hers too."

"And I insist on buying her the materials and accessories. A wedding present from me. I have a wonderful thought, why don't you paint their portrait?"

"We better get started with all this tomorrow, Rosie."

"Tonight. We'll start looking tonight."

"Fancy a pizza?"

"Chick flick, Anna?"

"Let's have ourselves a little party. There's no guests booked in for two more days; we can fill in at the B & B for now."

"I can do the cooking," Rosie offered.

"That's best, I've already got the rooms covered. I'm a dab hand."

Bear barked, just to remind them he was there, and far too big to get in unless they opened the door!

"Aww. Sorry, baby. I do hope you and Bumble are on the suitable list too."

"Did it say anything about puppies or kittens, just saying?" Anna laughed.

"You let my dog in, I'm going to lock up these papers. Then we can sit and look at styles."

Rosie almost skipped down to the basement. She didn't *want* to know everything. Dorothea had told her enough, for now. Things were about to get very interesting in Bromington-on-sea, her future and everyone else's was bright.

At least, she hoped so, it could be a dangerous thing knowing what was coming next if you couldn't do anything about it. What exactly *did* Dorothea know?

ABOUT THE AUTHOR

Trisha J. Kelly is an author living in Norfolk, UK. She is a multi-genre writer with quite a few published books available on Amazon and several more due for release in the future.

To date she has written an award-winning middle-grade fantasy series for reading age approximately eight years and upwards. With many favourable five-star reviews from around the world. The books are equally enjoyed by adults and have generous comparisons to Enid Blyton and J. K. Rowling for the sheer imagination of the content. If you like magical adventures, quests and puzzles then jump onboard the totally unique Scarlett and Mason Series.

In order, the books are:

Discovering Witchetty Waters

In the Wrong Lifetime

The Rise of Sorcha

When Some Were Missing

The Great Storm of 1397

The Mystery of the Ancient Key

Staying with books for even younger children, Trisha has also published two more books. Again, these are suitable for a younger audience with help from an older reader.

24 Sleeps to Go is an adorable book of short, but filling Advent stories. One Christmas themed tale for every night from the 1ˢᵗ to the 24ᵗʰ December. A special keepsake and countdown to Christmas that children will love being read to them, or they can read for themselves. Trisha hopes to bring out a second book of *24 Sleeps to Go – Edition two* in 2019.

Keeping with the Christmas theme and young readers of eight and over, Trisha also released a wonderful Christmas story entitled *Blinky, Nutkins and Friends.* When a group of forest animals team up with an eccentric professor and his pets anything is possible as they set off in search of Santa's Village.

For the older readers, Trisha has released a wonderful mystery, the first in the series of cold cases regarding missing people, intertwined with fresh murders along the way. Intricate plots laced with plenty of humour.

A Tropical Murder is available on Amazon and will be followed up with *A Lakeside Murder* then *A Campsite Murder.*

Not stopping there, Trisha has also published a gritty two book series of crime thrillers.

Harry's Secrets and *The Conflict* are both available on Amazon, and again, have some very good 5* reviews. Trisha has shown her adaptability in her writing styles by producing two addictive books favourably compared to Martina Cole and Mandasue Heller.

Trisha is being a touch modest, readers, well... why not read the reviews! Follow Trisha for news of all her latest releases.

https://www.amazon.co.uk/Trisha-J.-Kelly/e/B06XHJZPDP

For a peak inside some of the books, you can find Trisha's website here:

https://www.trishajkellypublications.co.uk/

Also, in the pipeline and coming your way soon, more books in the brand new Wodehouse Mysteries. Follow Rosie and the other characters in the upcoming cases.

'The Tones of War'. Historical fiction coming in 2019. Follow some East End families as they live through the horrors of WWII. Also, see the second world war through the eyes of the painter. A man given the responsibility of taking in two evacuees.

Coming up also; a YA trilogy. Follow Wynter and the trials and tribulations of The Econians. A race of people trapped in another existence. Among them a father the heroine has never met. *Wynter* will be the first book of the Econian Legend series, followed by *Helena* and *Artemus*.

Not stopping there, if horror is right up your street, then hide behind your cushions and sleep with the lights on. *Silence* will be sure to chill you to your bones. Coming soon.

Why not connect with Trisha on social media. She runs a group for indie authors and moderates and administrates on others.

Thank you for reading a little about her books and please, reviews are always very welcome for any writer.

https://www.facebook.com/TrishajkellyAuthor/

https://twitter.com/Trishajkelly

Printed in Great Britain
by Amazon